Kè Su Thar was born in 1965, in Aung Lan, a small town of Burma (Myanmar). His parents were so poor that they could not afford to school him. Hence, his formal education ended early in his childhood, in primary level. However, he never gave up learning. He taught and groomed himself.

He has written some short stories and three novels—*Karzu, Forgotten Biography* and *His Day*—all in Burmese. His short stories have appeared in some magazines. This is his first novel written in English. Now he lives in Yangon with his elder sister's family.

To my mother, the first good storyteller in my life.

Kè Su Thar

THE FILM

AUSTIN MACAULEY PUBLISHERS™
LONDON • CAMBRIDGE • NEW YORK • SHARJAH

Copyright © Kè Su Thar (2019)

The right of Kè Su Thar to be identified as author of this work has been asserted by him in accordance with section 77 and 78 of the Copyright, Designs and Patents Act 1988.

All rights reserved. No part of this publication may be reproduced, stored in a retrieval system, or transmitted in any form or by any means, electronic, mechanical, photocopying, recording, or otherwise, without the prior permission of the publishers.

Any person who commits any unauthorized act in relation to this publication may be liable to criminal prosecution and civil claims for damages.

A CIP catalogue record for this title is available from the British Library.

ISBN 9781788786218 (Paperback)
ISBN 9781788786225 (Hardback)
ISBN 9781788786232 (E-Book)

www.austinmacauley.com

First Published (2019)
Austin Macauley Publishers Ltd
25 Canada Square
Canary Wharf
London
E14 5LQ

The first three chapters of this novel, in a somewhat different form, appeared in *Be Untexed*, a Burma-based online journal of new writings and visual arts. For this, I thank the editors of the journal.

My special thanks go to my niece, Theint, for helping me financially to finish and publish this book, and to artist Maung Di for encouraging me to publish this book.

Author's Note

This is fiction. However, everything in this fiction is based on facts. Hence, this is fiction based on facts. In other words, this is fact-based fiction.

This is what I see through the peeping hole of my mind when I am silent in the long silence with no thought in it.

Kè Su Thar

Table of Contents

Chapter I   11
This Is What I See

Chapter II   35
Through the Peeping Hole

Chapter III   57
Of My Mind

Chapter IV   80
When I Am Silent

Chapter V   108
In the Long Silence

Chapter VI   138
With No Thought in It

Chapter I
This Is What I See

"I star as a translator in this film."
The words slip out, breaking the dead silence in the room.
How did they slip out? Why did they slip out?
No doubt that those words may be the answer to a question. And who did answer?
It is very hard for me to accept that I am the one who answered. I tell myself that it might be someone else who replied. I tell myself that I overheard someone else say, or that what I really spoke was something completely different from what I really heard or that I spoke nothing, but I was deceived by my mind and ears into thinking that I spoke. I tell myself that I really did not hear anything, yet I was deceived by my mind or ears into thinking that I heard. Does this mean that I suffer from hallucinations? No, no, no. I am sane. I am mentally healthy. I can see things clearly as they are, not as they appear to be. However, now nothing is clear to me. Is it possible that I have no data in my mind of what I really said? I must confess that these words shocked me a lot, and I try to pretend that I remain calm or that nothing can make me panicky. Like someone who is being haunted by the soul of the person he murdered, I am being haunted by what I did not say.
I am not sure whether my eyes can conceal my emotions, because I know well that I am not good at acting, and I never tried to be good at acting. If my eyes fail, then it will become very easy for others to read my mind, and they will come to spot the things in my mind.
I have no idea what will happen to me next, within a few seconds. I sense that I look like the one who is trying to flee from

something wrong he has done. I don't like such type of guys. But who can say that I am not such type of a guy? You?

Some questions are making such a loud buzzing noise in my mind that I can no longer swallow, and I urge myself that I must ask questions to stop the noise. Whom must I ask? Who will answer? Anyway, I have no chance to shun this situation. (Does this mean that what is happening to me now is a part of my destiny?) Before asking myself other questions, I think of the words: **star, translator, film**. I think I am familiar with the meanings of all these words. But I am not sure from where I learnt these words. Anyway, I must confess that I know the real definition of these words.

According to the context here, **star** means, 'to play the most prominent or important role in a movie or play'. And now you must have knowledge of what the words – **play**, **prominent**, **important**, **role**, **movie**, and **play** – mean.

And what is **translator**? To know what **translator** means, you must know first what **translate** means. According to the definition of Merriam-Webster, **translate** means, 'to turn into one's own language or another language'. And now you must have knowledge of what the words – **turn into**, **own**, **language**, and **another** – imply.

Then in your memory, the word **film** and its meaning must have been kept well. According to the definition of Merriam-Webster, **Film** is 'motion picture'. And what does **motion picture** mean? Merriam-Webster defines **motion picture** as 'a series of pictures projected on a screen in rapid succession with objects shown in successive positions slightly changed so as to produce the optical effect of a continuous picture in which the objects move'. Then Merriam-Webster shares another word for **motion picture**. It is, 'movie'.

Accordingly, you must have at least 34 words and their denotation in your memory so that you can seize what the sentence "I star as a translator in this film" (I overheard or I really uttered) really means.

I have no idea of what her question was. In reality, it is my right to know her question and the intention of her question. Don't you think that it makes no sense that both the question and its intention are hidden from me? Don't you think that it is unjust to have to answer the question without knowing what it is and what its intention is? Or don't you think that it is ridiculous not to be able to remember the question even if I had the right to know it? Was I forced and bullied to do so? I don't think that I was fooled into doing this, because I am not an idiot. Is it true that I myself have answered? I don't want to accept the fact that I gave this answer. And if you ask me whether I did, my answer is: no I didn't. If it is reality, then it will be no use to deny doing this. And I must keep silent. Here, in this case, keeping silent means that I am an actor, doesn't it?

What is real is what is real, whether you accept it or not. You can't change it at all.

Have you ever done such a fucking thing in your life? Here I happen to use the word *life*, which I always fail to see clearly. Even though I use the word *life* occasionally, I don't really know its meaning well. My knowledge about life is very superficial. To me, life is something like a dream with neither beginning nor ending. Once I tried to look up the word *life* in a dictionary, and found that the definition is not what I hope to see. The definition is so superficial. And so, sometimes, I think about the terms *being* and *existence* as well. If you are interested in philosophy you will be familiar with the above-mentioned terms. Those terms also have their definitions and explanations. So to know what they really refer to we need to have certain knowledge about their definitions and explanations. However, definitions and explanation are just definitions and explanations, not more than that. They can't cover reality. To know definitions and explanations is one thing and to realize reality is the other thing. To define a word, many words are used. The first result is that we get many words. And the second result is that we are farther from reality. Even when I use the word *reality* I have never seen it, never experienced it. I am like a poor boy who sells apples, but never bites an apple. Now I find myself trying to tell you about the taste of an apple. Certainly reality is not an apple.

At any rate, I am sure that, unintentionally, I committed a mistake against my will. Am I the type of a person who always commits this mistake or that mistake against my will? How many mistakes have I made in my life? I should remember the things I have done—good or bad—to judge what type of a guy I was or am. Things in my past have been taken out of my memory, haven't they? It is too bad. What does it like to be a person without memory of his past? I, like everyone, have my own past. I was born. I was nurtured. I was educated. No doubt at all, it is clear. But I don't remember my past. Now my memory is like a hard-disk which is so severely damaged by a virus that it lost its information. Or my memory is like a hard-disk the data of which has been totally deleted by reformatting. What can I do about it? Can I repair it? The answer is no. What a painful thing!

Do you hope that I will cry out like the one who is shipwrecked? No, I will not. It is not because I don't need someone's help in this room, but because I don't believe in anyone in this room.

I try to calm down myself and see things clearly. What is wrong with me? The questions occur to me before I can stop them. Do I forget that I am an actor? Do I forget that I answered: *I star as a translator in this film*?

Can I say that I said nothing?

From those words, you may judge that I must be an actor, especially, *star as* implies that I am an actor. The problem is this: I don't feel that I am an actor. I know well what an actor is, what a good actor is. Even among my friends, some are good actors. I am sure I am not interested in acting. I admire some actors and actresses. I admire the art of acting. But this does not suggest that I am an actor, or I want to be an actor. I don't think that the dream to ever be an actor occurred to me even once. That is why I must be insisting that I am not an actor. Damn it! I have told again that I am not an actor.

I don't even know how I am here. I fancy that I had never seen the young woman in a grey uniform, sitting on the small stool-like sofa in front of me. Who is she? What is she? How and why is she with me here in this large room? And how and why am I here with her in this large room? Is she real or imaginary? I don't dare to believe even my sensory perception. Our perceptions are unreliable; they sometimes try to fool us into mistaking something unreal for something real, or vice versa.

Complete silence in the room. No sound, no voice but those of my words in my mind. The room seems to be waiting for something wrong I am going to commit. I find myself friendly with the atmosphere of the room, but I can't find any clue in my memory about how many times I have ever frequented this room. My memory tells me that this is the first time I sit on this sofa, in this room, which is the largest one I have ever seen. However my feeling tells me that this is not the first time I sit on this sofa, in this room. What is right? What my memory tells or my feeling tells? If the former is right, the latter must be wrong. If the former is wrong, the latter will be right. Can both be right? Can both be wrong? Impossible.

Sitting on the sofa, I scan everything around me in silence, with the hope that something I see will be able to explain to me what is happening to me or with the hope that I will see something which can give my memory back. I still harbor the feeling that I will be able to find out my real identity in some ways. Strangely, at the same time, I harbor doubt about my ability.

I see four camera operators—a young man and three young women—shooting our interview or conversation (I prefer the word *conversation* to the word *interview* here; what's more I feel that this is a conversation, not an interview, therefore I will use the word *conversation* later) from different angles. Does a conversation need to be shot like this? They look like robots which are so identical to humans. I don't trace even a faint expression on their faces. Even when my eyes meet with theirs, their eyes show no sign of seeing me. It seems that they were not educated to express their feelings and emotions or it seems that they were educated to suppress or conceal their feelings and emotions. I am disappointed. In their eyes, I seem to be an inanimate object which is so identical to a human.

She asks questions. I give answers. But sometimes I don't answer to her questions; I ask counter-questions instead. It seems that she has already asked me a lot of questions and I have given a lot of answers to her. The problem is that I can't recall anything—what questions she has asked me and what answers I have given her.

I have no second thought that this conversation is very important not only to me but to them. I have no idea why I am so sure like that. Maybe it is my basic instinct that helps me detect this. However, my basic instinct obviously fails to inform me about the real trap from which I can't escape. Unintentionally, I happened to use the word *trap*. This confirms that I see this situation as an unpleasant one. It is time to ask myself whether I feel annoyed, perplexed, irritated etc. My answer is: no. At present, I can't say anything but that I don't like this situation. This does not mean that I feel the atmosphere of danger.

Two men are busy with the arrangement of light. I am aware that I have knowledge of lighting during a shoot. It is certain that my memory has kept the knowledge of lighting. I wonder why. Is it because I have read some books on lighting or is it because I have experience of arranging lighting? The other questions occur to me. Why have I read such books? Why do I have such experiences?

Titles of some books occur to me: *Film Lighting*, *Lighting for Cinematography*, *Set Lighting Technicians Handbook*, *Lighting for Film and TV Productions, The Technique of Lighting for Television and Film*, *Lighting for TV and Fil*m etc. Have I read all these books? It is impossible. So why are these titles in my memory? No answer. There must be a relationship between those books and me. The problem is that it is a secret. It is deniable that I have some knowledge of film and lighting. I am not sure if I have read all of them, yet I am sure that I have some experience of arranging lighting. Are the causes hidden here?

Maybe I have friends in the field of film and television. And maybe all this knowledge comes from them. I must thank my memory for it kept the titles of the books well in it. I am not sure if all these titles are correct.

I remember well that I have watched a lot of TV conversations. Some of them are very interesting, yet most of them are boring, not like the real ones, but like the conversation scenes in the films starring poor actors and actresses. And is this, too, one scene of conversation in a film? I can't say 'yes' or 'no' definitely; I don't feel certain that everything I see or hear, smell or touch, feel or imagine now is real. Is the conversation false? Or am I false? Or is something false? Or is everything false? FALSE FALSE FALSE FALSE FALSE FALSE FALSE FALSE FALSE FALSE FALSE. What false is false.

All people in the room—including the young woman sitting in front of me, the four camera operators, and others—are robot-like. All actions they perform—how they move from here to there, how they handle things, how they adjust their camera tripods, how they focus their cameras on me, on her, how they take position, how they communicate each other with gestures or words—are like those which robots do. I detect no feeling, no emotion, and no expression in their eyes, in their actions, in their gestures, in their manners. Straight-faced they are; poker-faced they are. There must be certain causes behind this. The causes are hidden.

Do we have password to gain access to the system of these hidden causes? Imagine that we have password. What would we see if we entered the password?

I, with the hope that she will smile back at me, smile at a young woman who is helping the female camera operator position her camera tripod. My eyes and her eyes meet. Her eyes show no sign of seeing me, as if she sees nothing, as if she sees only vast space. She is an energetic young woman of about twenty-two or so. She has red cheeks, red hair and bright, wide eyes, like those of a cat. I assume that she is an ambitious young woman. If my prediction is not wrong, she will become a successful camera operator one day. I forget that I can't even predict what will happen to me the next second or the next minute.

All of them are working with great care, with extreme caution. Are they being afraid that they will make a slight mistake? Are they working as exactly as commanded? Are they being under control of someone? I don't want to blame them; I don't want to find fault in them. I don't want to despise them. I have no idea under whose supervision or control they are working. I have no idea for which channel they are working. Perhaps they are freelance filmmakers. None of them is my acquaintance, yet I don't feel that any of them is a stranger to me. The young woman in front of me, too, is not my acquaintance; possibly this is the first time that I meet her and that she interviews me. I, however, don't have any feeling that she is an unfamiliar person. Though I have nothing about her in my memory, I feel that maybe she is my friend or my friend's friend.

I don't say that I have a very *excellent* memory, yet I do say that I can remember some events even from my childhood in great detail, exactly as I experienced then. Majority of the events in my childhood are still vivid in my mind. If I say that I remember well what happened to me when I was four, you might think I am lying. Even my childhood friends, when I told them about our childhood, were amazed, and thought that those real stories were my invented stories of our childhood, because they all have no memory of what I tell them.

Now I am going to tell you a story of my early life as exactly as I underwent then. If what I kept in my memory remains untainted, what I recall will be the same as what happened to me. If what I recall is the same as what happened to me, what I am going to tell you now will be true.

Now you can see a thirteen-year-old boy in your imagination. He was not sharp. He was not hopeful. He was not upbeat. He was not strong and well-built. He was thin and short. He was always bullied by big guys of his own age, who were well-built than he was. He always felt inferior among other students. However, he never failed to conceal his fear.

The boy had no knowledge of his birth parents. Maybe it was because his foster parents never told him about them or he dared not to ask them about his birth parents. He did not even know that he was a foster child before he started to go to middle school. No doubt that his foster parents loved him so much. He was amazed to know the truth of his life, because he never hoped that he was abandoned by his birth parents. He never conceived how a child would feel when he found himself as an abandoned child. Being abandoned by birth parents is worse than one can imagine.

From whom did he learn it? Possibly it was from a man or a woman who knew everything about his childhood that he came to learn it. Even the thought to ask his foster parents about how he was deserted by his birth parents and how he became their adopted child never occurred to him; he pretended that he knew nothing about it.

However, he could not help asking himself questions about fate or destiny or fatalism or determinism. There is no question that he, being a baby, could do nothing bad to his natural parents, but he was abandoned. Why? Was it because he was ugly? Was it because a certain fortuneteller predicted that he might bring ill luck? His birth parents seemed to sell him to his foster parents or his foster parents seemed to find him somewhere as an abandoned baby, and fostered him. Another possible story is that his biological parents died a few days or a few months or a few years after his birth, and so he was adopted by others. Whenever he watched *The Curious Case of Benjamin Button*, he thought that some parts of his life looked like those of Benjamin Button, yet he was not a curious bloke whose life was not as interesting as that of Benjamin Button. Sometimes he missed his birth parents even though he could not form their images in his mind. Sometimes he imagined that he grew up, living with them. What might be the difference? If they were poor, he would be poor. If they lived a hand-to-mouth existence, he would live hand-to-mouth, too. If they could not afford to school him, he might not have chance to go to school. He would not get even a so-called university degree awarded by 'state education' of his country. Instead he would remain uneducated. He would be a laborer, a construction worker or a hawker or a gangster etc. Whenever he met such child workers in construction sites or in street tea shops, he thought that his life would be like theirs if he was not adopted. It would be hard for him to be free from being molded by the environment where he grew up. He would be a certain type of guy as shaped by the environment where he was raised.

His foster parents were very strict disciplinarians, and he was raised under their strict guidance. The result was that he became a courteous man, a law-abiding citizen.

Though he knew this secret, he kept it as it was. He never felt that he was their adopted son. He never had seen even a slight sign on their faces that they fostered him. They always treated him as their birth child because to them he was a birth child. He loved them so much; he admired them so much. He was proud of being their son. Sometimes he doubted the fact that he was adopted. He thought that perhaps he was fooled.

He had a friend. She always tried to understand him. Whenever he felt downhearted, she always solaced him. Indeed she was not only his friend but his counselor. She was his good adviser. She was an avid reader. At her home, there was a small library, and so it was a great treasure for her. She told him about the tales she read. It was from her that he heard the tales of Ali Baba, of Aladdin etc. He never forgot the wonderful lamp. When he was young, he wanted to have such a wonderful lamp to fulfill his wishes with the help of the magical power of the lamp.

When he told about his imagination, she gave a light laugh.

"Oh, great," she acclaimed and said. "I dreamt I had a magic lamp which can make my imagination come true. With the help of the lamp, I make myself a princess. And you are my bodyguard."

"I am your bodyguard!"

"Of course, you are." She gave a side glance to me, and then she asked, "Don't you want to be my bodyguard?"

"No, I don't mean so. I want to be your bodyguard. Really I want. I am afraid you will not appoint me to guard you."

She giggled.

He was happy to see her laugh.

If I had a chance to look into a mirror then I would see my expression, and then I would be able to check my emotion.

Perhaps, we are in the middle of a conversation. Perhaps she is the one who leads the conversation. As I have mentioned above, I have no memory of how many questions she's asked me and how many answers I've given her. I can't imagine why I was not aware of this just before now. It could be that I have been sitting, unconscious. Or it could be that I have been in a deep sleep. Seemingly, something made me unaware of what was happening to me. Now it is time for me to wake up. It is time for me to be conscious of everything I undergo. I will be aware of every question she will ask. I will be conscious of every answer I will give. I will be aware of everything she will tell me. I will be conscious of everything I will tell her. What's more, I will be aware of everything I will think of.

I look swiftly at the young woman, whose name I don't know, whose impeccable manner I admire. She does not look at me. She is looking at the vast space outside the room in a thoughtful manner. She is thinking of something deeply.

"Well, I have some more questions," she says suddenly, coming out of her deep thoughts, taking one abrupt look at me. "I hope you'll have some more time to answer my questions." Her tone of voice uncovers her self-confidence.

I remain silent, because I don't know what to tell her. I am not sure whether I have time to answer her questions as freely as I want. She seems to be waiting for my reply: 'yes' or 'no'. In reality, my reply is not so important. What is important is that I should have the right to ask her some questions.

"Am I an actor?" I am about to ask her the question. But I fail, because something I don't expect occurs to me and prevent me from asking.

"You've studied how a translator leads his life, haven't you?" she says, without waiting for my reply. Her question wakes me up, shaking my sleepy condition of mind.

My answer is, "Of course, I've."

For what did I study how a translator leads his life? I don't believe my ears. Did I really say like that? I know well that what a translator is and how a translator leads his life. Maybe it is because some of my friends are translators. I don't think that I studied how a translator leads his life. But my answer confirms that I studied how a translator lives. Although I don't remember their names, I am sure that I have translator friends. Some translate Burmese writings into English, and some translate English writings into Burmese. Some live on translation. Some do not live on translation. Strangely, I know well that in our country it is hard to live on translating or writing. It is because majority of people do not read. If your book is sold 1,000 copies, you are a bestseller.

"Now for a short time let's change our subject," she announces.

I don't know why she wants to change the subject, but I agree.

"Some fans of yours say that you're an avid reader," she asks. "Are you really an avid reader?"

"Of course, I am," I answer. "How do they know it?"

"On the television, they watched the other interviews carried at your house, and they spot your book shelves full of several books."

The phrase 'other interviews' echoes in my mind. It means that this is neither the first nor the only conversation I have had and that one of those conversations was carried at my house. Oddly, in my memory, there is no information that I have made such conversations. Does this warn me that my memory is damaged slightly?

I have no idea what to say. How do they know that it was at my house that the interview was carried out? I have big book shelves full of books in my home library, so it may be true that they saw book shelves at my house. However, maybe it is not on the television that they saw them, but in my library at my house. Perhaps they paid a visit to my home and entered my library. Why did they visit to my home? Why did they enter my library?

How did they enter my home library? Without my knowledge or permission, no one can enter my library. There must be a certain reason for them to pay a visit to my house. There must be a certain reason for them to enter my home library. Somehow, they seemed to enter my home library. But I am sure that I never let anyone enter my home library. At least I should remember they paid a visit to my home even if I can't recall who they are and when they paid a visit. Now I find myself telling you about my house, and you may assume that I have a house in which a home library is located. In fact I can't even visualize either my house or my home library. Is it a large house or a small house? Is it a mansion or a bungalow? I am not sure. Is it a small home library or a huge home library? I am not certain. Besides, why do I have a large library? Even if I am an avid reader, it is hard to have a large library. I must be considerably rich enough to own a large library.

"They're right. I am an avid reader," I reply hesitantly. "I read a lot. I love books. I love knowledge and wisdom." I happen to stress the word 'knowledge' and the word 'wisdom' unintentionally.

"May I know what kind of books you read most?"

I shrug my shoulders, and say, "I have said that I love knowledge and wisdom." I cast a quick glance at her to see how she responds to what I have said. No expression on her face. I add, "But this does not mean that I am a philosopher. I am not interested in thinking."

"I'd like to know what kind of books you read most."

She is asking me questions like an officer is interviewing an applicant for a job. I hate bossy type. She is bossy. But I don't hate her.

"I am thinking of the answer. I feel that it is a question which is hard to answer in brief. I am afraid that my answer cannot cover the issue."

"Do you mean that you can't answer my question now?"

"Exactly."

"OK. No prob. At present, I'd like to know which book you are reading nowadays. I hope this is a simple question for you to answer."

I nod and say, "Of course, it is."

There is a silence between us. I am trying to think about the book I am reading now. Is it a novel or something? Why is it difficult for me to find out which book am I reading? Why do I forget the book I am reading now?

A title of something comes into my mind first. I don't know what it is. Is it a poem or a short story? Is it a novel or a memoir? Is it a play of a film?

Now I see a man lying in the dead leaves, like a corpse. His hair are matted. His face is grotesquely smudged and bruised. His clothes are in rags and are muddy. He hears the inhuman voice calling: "Attention, attention, attention." I see him turn his head. He tries to raise himself. He hears birds chanting: "Here and now, boys."

I have no idea who the man is.

The spectacle is still in my mind. It is an island.

I see two children: a girl and a boy. The girl is about six. Perhaps, the boy is one year younger than the girl. The boy is in a green loincloth. The girl is carrying a basket of fruit on her head. She is in a full crimson skirt. It reaches almost to her ankles. Above the waist she is naked. In the sunlight her skin glows like pale copper flushed with rose. Both are looking down at the man lying in the dead leaves. Their eyes are wide with astonishment and a fascinated horror.

Are these the things left in my memory after I have read a novel? Which novel? Is it the novel I am reading now? I don't think so. I think that I read it about five or six years ago. Some data in my memory is telling me that I took even some notes while reading it. But I can't recall. Where is the book in which I jotted down some notes? The note book is the evidence of the fact that I really read a novel. I have never seen the note book. In my memory the note book exists: outside, the note book does not really exist. What a curious thing!

It might be a dream. Maybe all I see—the girl, the boy, the man, and the island—are the things in the dream I had yesterday.

Sometime in the past, I used to ask myself if I had ever been to such islands, because I found myself on the island in dreams. In a dream I had six or seven years ago, I was making a stone sculpture at the bottom of the huge rock mountain. The rock mountain was so lofty that I couldn't see its top. Its top appears to penetrate the clouds in the sky. I imagined what would be there on the other side of the mountain. I wanted to climb the mountain to see the things on its top. I was not sure whether I managed to climb the top of the lofty mountain or I spent time, looking up at it. If the data in my memory is right, it is certain that seven or eight years ago I wrote a novella about a scholar who tried to flee from the island of barbarians. I remember the whole plot of the novella in detail. The scholar did not know what kind of scholar he was. He did not remember how he was there on the island. When he found, gems, he knew they are gems. He knew well that he did not belong to the barbarians on the island. If time and everything permit, I will tell you this story.

And so I doubt that everything I experience now. I sense that I am having a dream which is identical to the real. Strangely, nothing I experience now fazes me at all. I feel ease. I feel comfort. I feel free.

"Sometimes I find it hard to distinguish dreams from reality," I tell our young woman, who is absorbed in something. She seems to be thinking about something serious. Maybe she is preparing other difficult questions to ask me. She does not seem to hear my words. Or maybe she pretends not to hear my words. And I say the same words aloud. She lifts her head suddenly and looks at me. No sign on her face. Surely she heard nothing. It is impossible. I said clearly and loudly. If I really said, certainly she would hear. Didn't I say anything? If so, why did I think that I said?

I shake my head. And I try to drive it out. *I said nothing. I thought nothing*, I say in my mind.

With a faint smile on my face, I say, "I have no second thought about what I have experienced." This is not what I had intended to say. What I had really wanted to say was something else. But I can't do anything; I have already said. I can't take back the words I have already spoken.

She gives me a confused look, which warns me that what I said is not absolutely related to her question, and reminds me that I fail to answer her question. I forget to answer her question. Damn it! What a careless idiot! No, great! What a clever guy!

I have no idea what she is thinking. I have no interest in what she is thinking. Maybe she thinks that I am an idiot who does not obey social rules. Maybe she thinks that I am impolite.

I see me standing by an old woman on her deathbed and a young woman, who is telling her to do everything lightly. I am familiar with the denotation of the word *lightly*. In what sense she is using the word *lightly*. I don't know. Anyhow I think I get what it means here. I feel slight lightness in my heart. Life is light, isn't it? While examining what they two are doing, I fancy that I come to experience the taste of life and death.

And I hear the young woman say lightly, "Remember what you used to tell me when I was a little girl: 'Lightly, child, lightly. You've got to learn to do everything lightly. Think lightly, act lightly, feel lightly. Yes, feel lightly even though you're feeling deeply. Just lightly let things happen and lightly cope with them.' I was so preposterously serious in those days, such as humorless little prig. Lightly, lightly—it was the best advice ever given me."

What I hear is so clear. I look around to find the narrator. At that time, I hear her say.

"Well, now I'm going to say the same thing to you. Lightly, my darling, lightly. Even when it comes to dying. Nothing ponderous, or portentous, or emphatic. No rhetoric, no tremolos, no self-conscious persona putting on its celebrated imitation of Christ or Goethe or Little Neil. And, of course, no theology, no metaphysics. Just the fact of dying and the fact of the Clear Light. So throw away all your baggage and go forward. There is quicksand all about you, sucking at your feet, trying to suck."

I think I know who she is. The problem is that I can't recall her name. At any rate, I know these things about her. She is beautiful. She is gentle. She is wise. She has modest manner. She has self-confidence. She has self-esteem.

She is not in grey uniform. Maybe she is the daughter-in-law of the old woman who is on her deathbed. I feel her light tone of voice.

Why do I find myself standing by her? Though I am standing by her, she does not seem to see me at all. When she turns her face towards me, I smile at her with the hope that she will say something to me. Vain hope. No reaction to my smile. She shows no sign of seeing me.

As mentioned above, I admire her tone of voice, which is clear and pleasant to hear, even though she is a bossy type.

"I think you have not answered my question," the young woman in grey uniform says.

I nod. "Terribly sorry," I reply in a hurry. "I think I am reading *Things Apart*."

"Is it a novel?"

"No, a memoir."

"Whose?"

I can't recall the name of the author though I try to remember. Finally I tell her a name. It is a lie, a crime.

She looks at me, with a puzzled expression on her face.

"I am afraid; I have never read his writings."

From what I see and hear, from the situation in which I am, I must accept that she is the interviewer and I am the interviewee. I am not sure how many interviews (If you have a good memory, you will remember that I have said that I prefer the word 'conversation' to the word 'interview' here; what's more I feel that this is a conversation, not an interview, therefore I will use the word 'conversation' later; but now I must use the word 'interviewer', 'interviewee' and 'interview') I had already given. I don't think that I am such a celebrated person to give an interview. However, it is undeniable that I am giving an interview here and now. From this, it can be concluded that I am a celebrated person.

I don't understand what I myself have said. I swear that I am not pretending to be an actor. I swear that I am not giving the interview with a will. I myself can't believe the fact that I am being interviewed is real. Anyway, it is sure that I am familiar with the word 'interview' and its denotation. This proves that I have learnt the word from somewhere. Moreover, I have knowledge that the word 'interview' was used as the title for a film about two American reporters and North Korean dictator, Kim Jong-un.

"Did I say that I star as a translator in this film?" This is what I want to ask the young female interviewer, who is thinking of the next questions to ask me.

Now she says nothing. She is silent as if she has nothing to say. From the signs in her eyes, I am aware that she keeps something secret: I don't know exactly what it is.

My mind, without my notice, goes back to the opening sentence, and the questions occur to me one after another. Why don't I remember the question she asked me? Am I being prevented from remembering the important facts of my life? Is everything I remember within limits? If I am allowed to remember A, I remember A. If I am not allowed to remember B, I do not remember B. That's all. I have no chance to choose. I have no right to choose. I have no power to choose. Why don't I have the chance? Why don't I have the right? Why don't I have the power? Why can I do nothing? Doesn't my memory belong to me?

I am aware that I feel upset. I should not let this happen. I shake my head, and try to calm myself. I seem to have the practice of calming myself down. My mind gradually becomes settled, balanced. And I try to give up finding out the question: I sense that it might be a trap for me. The sentence "What is your role in this film?" might be the question for the sentence "I star as a translator". It might be that there are the other possible questions. Well, I don't try to know the question before this one: I am tired of thinking.

In the room some people are being busy with their jobs or they are pretending to be being busy. I try to communicate with them, gesturing. I am sure they see me. But they don't respond to my gesture. This means that they don't see me or that they pretend not to see me. I resent.

I don't want to know the beginning of this conversation, but I do want to know what and who I am. Are the events I recall connected to my real life? Is everything I remember false? Do I forget the real facts related to my real life? Do I take false events as real events? Even though I try to stop asking myself questions, questions arise against my will.

"Do you know who and what I am?" I ask the young woman.

She shows no expression of hearing what I asked her. From this, I will not judge that my voice was so low that she could not hear. I sense that she heard what I asked her. I can't give a reasonable explanation to this. All I can say is that I feel that she is only pretending not to hear my question. It is not from her expression that I detected her pretention, but from my innate ability. The expression on her face confirms that she did not hear what I told her. But from my innate ability, surely, she heard what I told her.

My memory does not work well enough to remember the events of the nearest past—one or two minutes ago. I, however, know the word 'translator' and its meaning. What's more, I even know the other words which collocate with this word: 'poetry translator', 'short story translator', 'essay translator', 'fiction translator', 'novel translator' etc. Even if I am an actor who stars as a translator, I am not sure what kind of translator I am in this film. It is strange that I feel that I have ever read a novel which opens with an interview and the plot of which I fail to remember. Am I the one who wrote it? Impossible!

I don't want to ask any questions, but things drive me into questioning this or that, these or those. Must I say yes to the fact that what is happening to me now is real? Must I try to find out reality? To say yes is easy: to find out reality is hard. There are so many barriers. There are so many hidden facts. There are so many obstacles. If what is happening to me is not real, what is real? If what is happening to me is real, how about the stories of my life I kept in my memory? Are they not real? Why do I doubt everything I experience in this very room?

Something tells me that I have a chance to come out of this dilemma. Bravo!

Whether everything I go through is real or not, whether I am an actor or not, whether I star as a translator in a film or not, surely I know what an actor is, I know what a leading character is, I know what a translator is, I know I am not an actor, and I know I am not a translator. But in my memory, I have titles of some novels written in English or translated into English: *The Man in the Dark Room, The Mysterious Flame of Queen Loana, A Prayer for Owen Meany, The Unbearable Lightness of Being, Karnaf Café*, etc. It might be that all these novels seem to be those which I have read, not those which I have translated into Burmese.

According to vague recollection, before I started acting as a translator in the film, I had spent some months with some famous translators so that I would be familiar with the real character of a translator. I don't remember the names of the translators with whom I spent time. I am not sure what I learnt from them. However, I am familiar with the life of a translator. Is this the proof that I am an actor who, for his role in a new film, tried to learn how a translator leads his life?

I remember a Burmese actress who studied some mentally ill women in the asylum for her character in a film.

As an actor or as a novelist or as a general reader, I have read some biographies and autobiographies of famous actors and actresses. As an actor or as a novelist or as a general reader, I have watched some bio-cinemas of famous actors and actresses. I remember those biographies and autobiographies I have read. I remember those bio-cinemas I have watched. But I don't remember the films in which I starred. If I am really an actor, I should remember the films in which I starred.

It seems that my only dream was to be a novelist. I seemed to study the art of fiction writing. I seemed to read books on the art of writing. I can tell you about the books of fiction writing. I can tell you about the books on the art of writing. But I am not sure whether they are the books I've read or not. They might be the books I read or the books about which my novelist friends told me about.

I am not sure whether I am actor or not, but I am sure that I am a big fan of films. And I remember that I have read some books on films, though I have no aim to be a director or a scripter writer or an actor. *Surrealist Cinema* is one of the books on films which I have already read. Now I am writing a novel about a movie star, who died about six years ago. No one was with him when he died. He loved living alone. He loved solitude. Most of the films in which he starred were surrealist. His life was surreal as well. In an interview he said, "My life is dream-like. Everything which happened to me is what I never hoped, expected or predicted. I never dreamt of becoming a famous actor. It seems that a certain agent is running my life, I think. But I am not sure what it is. What I mean is that my life runs not as directed or planned by me, but as directed or planned by something powerful which I can't identify. You can call it what you like."

I have not decided whether I should put this in my book about him, because it is related to determinism or fatalism. But I have a view that there is something beyond our knowledge, beyond our control, beyond our power. What we can do is within a limit, within what we are allowed to do. Whenever I think of our limited power or powerlessness, I remember Jesus' words: "The hour has come, and the Son of Man is betrayed into the hands of sinners." Am I passive? This is the question haunting me all the time.

Since ten years ago I have already watched *Red Balloon*, a 13-minute thriller film, directed by Alexis Wajsbrot and Damien Mace. I like it so much. The other short film I like is *My Friend's Home* directed by Kim Hak-min, Kin Sol, and Ahn Jeong-hyun.

I have already watched some movies, such as *Beautiful Mind, Seven Samurai, Life Is Beautiful, Pretty Baby, Jacob the Liar, La Argue, Black Swan, Returning Home, The Angriest Man* etc. I, having a good memory, can remember the plot of every film I have watched. Maybe this is what I inherited from my parents. My father could remember anything he had read once. My mother could retell nearly everything she went through in her life. She had many stories she learned from her life. She was a good story-teller. I promise that in later parts I will tell you my mother's stories if I will not forget to tell you or if I will not break my promise.

The other precious thing I inherited from my mother is the ability to show tolerance towards the things, good or bad, I undergo. My parents were poor, so I had no chance to have a formal education. As far as I can recall, I felt sorry and inferior in my childhood and boyhood. Later, my mother's teachings strengthened and encouraged me.

When I started to write the novel about an actor, my girlfriend advised me that I should not write such a novel because I had no knowledge of an actor or an actress. Here we should take into consideration the fact that I have a girlfriend. From this, it can be concluded that I have a girlfriend. Who is she? What is she? Is she tall or short? Is she pretty or ugly? Is she intelligent or stupid? I can't imagine anything. Everything is vague. It might be that I have a girlfriend, but I have no memory of her. As far as I can recall, she is not fat, she is not short, she is not stupid, and she is not arrogant. Then I suspect what I can recall about her. I see her as a perfect, young woman. Is she a perfect, young woman?

OK, let her be like that.

She is right. But her words cannot stop my ideas and my eagerness to write it. Now I have already written nearly 100 pages. I don't know when I must end the novel. I am not sure whether even the opening part of my novel is like the opening part of a real novel.

My novel opens with the sentence: *The window opened.*

In my mind eyes, I saw a window open, and I wrote down the sentence: *The window opened.* That is all.

Later the opening sentence may change. But if it changes, the following sentences also may change, because the following sentences' contexts are related to it.

I have written some short stories, but this is the first novel, and I am not sure whether it will be published or not, whether I will be able to finish it or not. Probably I will stop writing it before it comes to an end. Then my unfinished novel will be lost secretly, and the facts in it also will be lost secretly. No one will have any knowledge that it really existed. No one will have knowledge about the facts in the novel.

To publish my novel, I must know a publisher; I must know a literary agent or a person like that. I don't know any publisher. I don't know any literary agent or an agent-like person. My girlfriend (this is the second time I use the phrase 'my girlfriend') told me that I should try to show my work to a literary agent. Indeed in my country there is no such agent but agent-like persons.

My girlfriend (this is the third time I use the phrase 'my girlfriend') is not only a good literary consultant but a harsh literary critic to me. Whatever I write, she is the first reader, the first editor, the first proofreader, the first critic. I always consult her. She always criticizes my writings. She always corrects my writings. She is a good reader. She is a good editor. She is a good critic. She never wrote a short story or an essay or a poem. She is too lazy to write. She never wrote a letter to me while she was in a remote region as a school teacher. She, however, is patient in reading. She reads everything closely.

"You're a good writer" is what she always tells me ironically. I know well what it really means. But I like it very much. And so I always reply, "Thank you, Madam."

There is a long silence in the room. I am silent as if I have nothing to say. In reality, I have so many things to say. My head is crammed with questions. I am astonished at my silence.

I star as a translator in this film, I say in my mind, and bitterly resent. I can't imagine why I fail to keep in mind everything that happened to me a few moments before I answered that I star as translator in this film. Have all facts in my memory been removed? Is it not logical that I don't know even the question she asked me? I have a belief that I have a considerably good memory. The events even in my childhood are still in my memory. Once I met with my childhood friends at a gathering and I retold them about what happened to us in our childhood, I saw some hints of astonishment on their faces. Am I the one whose memory is destroyed? Am I the one whose memory is excellent? Or am I the one who mistakes himself for someone else whose memory is excellent? Or am I the one who forgets that his memory is very bad?

I can't drive the vivid facts of the past out of my mind. No matter whether they are real or not, the conversation with my childhood friends really still exists in my memory.

My memory takes me to a certain past.

I was having a conversation with my childhood friend. He was a brave body, so he was called Brave Boy.

"Did we two really go on such adventures at the time?" Brave Boy asked after a long silence. His wide-opened eyes and the tone of his voice signified that he could not believe in what I told him. But he dared not to say that what I told him was not true, because he is one of my childhood friends who share the belief that my memory is very good.

We were talking about our childhood. One day the two of us played truant, and we went everywhere we wanted to. Only when we were tired, we came back home. Sometimes we ran. Sometimes we walked. When we were back at home, it was dark. My parents asked me what I did. And I told them everything I did. I did not conceal even the slightest thing. The result was that I was hit. The next evening, Brave Boy and I talked about our adventure and the great reward we got. Then we laughed hysterically.

I told Brave Boy about our great adventure. But he could not remember it at all. That is why he asked me such a question.

I have no habit of writing a diary; I am very lazy to write such a thing. Whenever I tell something about my childhood or boyhood I tell it from my memory, not from what I have written down in a diary. I never suspect what my memory tells me.

I have complete confidence in my memory. Now must I shatter my confidence myself? Does my memory not work well now? Even if my memory does not work well I am not ready to accept it as a fact, as a reality. Even if my memory fails to work properly, it remains good in my view.

I give a long sigh and stretch my body. I am convinced that I must be prepared for everything which may happen to me not as I expect, but as it will happen. Even this conversation is not what I have imagined. I have no idea why I am having such a fucking dull and boring conversation. I have no idea why I am sitting here to be interviewed as an actor. Damn it! I can't set myself free from this situation, can I?

The young woman seems to be very patient. I am not sure how many times I have met her. But I feel that I am very familiar with her. Maybe we have met several times before. I think that I am familiar with her tone of voice as well. It may be impolite if I ask her whether we have met before. She might get angry. I fear that she will be annoyed at my question. That is why I am keeping myself silent.

In a paragraph mentioned above, I have said that all people in the room are robot-like. Now I must correct my words. They are not robot-like. Maybe they are the victims of a certain illegal project. They are doing their duties exactly as commanded. She may also be the one who has to do her duty exactly as ordered. OK, then, ordered by whom? I remember someone told me that we were born as ordered or as planned. There is no order-maker; there is no plan-maker. There is no one who can order what I must do. There is no one who draws plans for my life. There is no one who governs my life. I seemed to tell someone that once before. Now I doubt my own words.

What if I will tell all these things to my interviewer?

"OK, let's restart our conversation," the young woman reminds me in a polite intonation and manner.

I don't know what she will ask. So I am not sure whether I can answer her questions.

I ask the young woman, "Have we ever met before?"

She answers nothing. Instead, she gives a strange look to me. Perhaps it means that she can't believe in what she hears and that it is the question she does not hope. If so, what is the question she hopes?

I suspect that the question I wanted to ask was one thing and the question I really asked was another. I suspect that it is only in my mind that I asked the question and I did not really ask any question to her out loud.

I notice that she starts typing.

It is a fruitful conversation. She pauses, and frowns. Then she continues.

From the way she moves her fingers on the laptop keyboard, I can say that she is very good at typing.

It seems that he is not ready for everything. It seems that it is hard for him to believe that what is happening to him is real. I see something strange in his eyes.

She is typing and typing. From what she has typed, I learn how she sees our conversation and me. Some facts do not agree with what we really talked about, but I don't criticize, not because I have no right, but because I don't want to.

Suddenly, she pauses typing, and gives me a blank expressionless look. I smile at her, but she does not return my smile.

Now she is checking what she has typed on the laptop screen.

Chapter II
Through the Peeping Hole

From what he has said, we can judge that he does not believe in love. Even having a good spouse is an obstacle for him. He has a lover. His fans want to know who his lover is. But it seems that he does not want to announce who she is. It might be that he has no intention of marrying her, or she has no intention to marrying him. All these are what she has typed.

I wonder why she typed so. I am not sure whether I answered that I did not believe in love. In fact, I have no idea what she asked me about love. Did she ask me whether I believe in love? If she asked me like that, my answer would be nothing but yes.

No matter what her question was. No matter what my answer was. It is wrong that she typed like that. I believe in love. Love is so powerful. Love can change the world. Love can build the world. Here the meaning of the word 'love' I refer may differ from that of the word 'love' she knows or the others know. We know *love* in our own ways. We define *love* in our own ways. Your knowledge about *love* might differ from my knowledge about *love*. Your definition of *love* might differ from my definition of *love*. In fact, I have many things to say about *love*. However, I can't. I must admit that I am like the one who has many stories to tell but is speech impaired.

According to what she has typed, I have a lover whom I don't want to marry or who does not want to marry me. I think, I should know whom and what she is. Is she beautiful or ugly? Is she generous or stingy? Is she educated or uneducated? Is she polite or rude? Is she intelligent or stupid? I know nothing about her. Don't you think that it is strange I know nothing about my lover?

I, with the hope of getting some hints of her thoughts, try to study the expression on her face without her knowledge. Surely she is lost in thought. Or it could be that she is like a hermit focusing her mind on a certain object. It might be that she is concentrating. Or it might be that she is meditating on something she has typed or what she will type. Does she have something to say about love? Does she have a boyfriend or a lover or a husband?

No one pays any attention to what we are talking. No one seems to be interested in our talk. No one seems to be curious. Curiosity seems to be a danger to them. Curiosity seems to be a trap to them. They seem to be afraid of curiosity or even the word 'curiosity'. Or their curiosity seemed to be crushed. That is bad.

My curiosity has not been crushed. It remains good. I want to know things. Sometimes I even want to know what others are thinking. I want to intrude their minds to investigate their thoughts. It is a certain type of hacking into other' minds. So it can be said that I am a mind-hacker. I know well that it is illegal. If so, let me ask: what is legal? Who does have power to judge what legal action is and what illegal action is? A certain action is legal according to a certain law. A certain action is illegal according to a certain law. And the question is: who makes laws? These thoughts are working in my mind. Are these thoughts legal or illegal? Is there a certain article of a certain law which allows these thoughts? Is there a certain article of a certain law which prohibits these thoughts?

A female name enters my mind. It is the name of the young woman in the grey uniform. She is the first interviewer.

The first interviewer is thinking of what happened to her in the past. Surely she had bad experiences in the past. Everything she underwent when she was young was a nightmare, and she can't imagine how she could bear and overcome every hardship. When she was a child, her mother died in prison. Her mother was a very strong political activist, a very strong-minded person like her grandfather on her mother's side. Her father is apolitical. But he did not forbid his wife to take part in political activity. Her father's second marriage after her mother's death made her hopeless, helpless, and she tried to commit suicide. Fortunately, or unfortunately, her attempt at suicide failed. From then onwards she came to see the light of life. She came to realize that her father's marriage to another woman was not abnormal, but normal. And in her eyes, her father became an ordinary father who lives as an ordinary human. But the trauma does not leave her. It remains rooted in a deep part of her mind.

In reality she wants to erase every data in her memory about her childhood, about her views of life, about her past. When her mother was in prison, she was belittled; she was despised; she was bullied. Fate was not on her side. The word 'fortunate' seemed to be a censored word for her. She had no playmate. No one dared to play with her. Even her cousins dared not to play with her. No one dared to go to school with her. Even her cousins dare not to go to school with her. No one dared to be friends with her. Even her cousins dared not to be friends with her. All shunned her as far as they could. She detected their fear in their eyes and in their actions. She, therefore, realized the nature of fear. Fear is a barrier to freedom. As far as she can recall, she felt lonely, but she did not feel depressed.

And now she was thinking about the meaning of life. Life is really a dream. Nothing more than a dream. She feels that she is in a dream.

Now she is thinking about me. She thinks that I am dodging some questions. She asked me a few minutes ago how I felt about my first film, in which I starred as a psychic murderer; I replied that I did not want to talk about things in the past. In reality, I am unsure whether I have starred as a psychic murderer in a film. I am not certain about my first film. To be exact, I have no idea about what she is talking about. That is why I gave such an answer. But she now thinks that I intentionally avoided her question, because I did not want to talk about it. Indeed, I have nothing to say about it. If I speak like that, my answer would be very rude, and she would be angry with me. My answer might be something which would beckon danger. Now I use the word 'danger' intentionally or unintentionally. Is this situation not a danger to me? At present, no one shows signs of aggression on their faces. But if I do or say something against the plan they've devised, I will surely be attacked by them.

To be honest, I don't like such characters. Whenever I watched the film about a psychic murderer, I felt uneasy. But it is strange that I can't help watching such films. Last month I read a novelette titled *Piercing*, and I felt restless. It was written by Ryu Murakami in Japanese and translated by a Burmese translator from English into Burmese. I did not read the original version or the English version. I read the Burmese version. It was my friend who advised me to read it. I don't know why I remember these things. I even remember the name of my friend who gave me a tip to read it. I even remember the Burmese title of the novelette. It is *Sue*. Are all these things real? Does my friend who advised me to read it really exists? Does Ryu Murakami really exists? Does the Burmese translator really exists? Are they—the writer, the translator, and my friend—the phantoms in my imagination? And what about *Piercing* and *Sue*? Are they the titles in my imagination? Is *Piercing* really the title of a novelette's English version? Is *Sue* really the title of a novelette's Burmese version? Did I really read it? Did I read it as an actor or as someone else? Or are all these things unreal? I must tell someone about *Piercing* or *Sue*, or about Ryu Murakami or Thint Lu, and ask him whether all those are real or not. Whom I must ask now? You? Or someone else?

Is there someone I can trust? Is there someone who loves justice? Is there someone who is detached? It is hard for me to have confidence in anyone now. I sense that everyone is trying to force me to accept the false fact that I am an actor. But maybe it is a fact that I am an actor, and it is a fiction that I sense so. If they are right, I will be wrong and surely I get paranoid.

I am unsure whether I really have intruded into her mind: it might be just a figment, too.

"Can you tell me what drove you to be an actor?"

"Nothing to say." This is what I want to say. What I really say is: "I had a dream to be an actor even in my boyhood."

"Oh, amazing, really amazing!" she exclaims.

I know it is just pretention. What I said is not something amazing.

I add, "However, I don't know why I had such a dream. I don't think that there was a reason. Actually I don't know the reason behind my dream to be an actor." While speaking so, I ask myself whether I am telling the truth or telling lies. Am I a good liar? I seem to be sure that I am not telling lies, that I am not a liar. If so, what am I? Am I an actor as they said? Am I someone else as I think? To certify that I am not an actor, I must have several documents. To certify that I am someone else, I must have several documents. Do they have documents to certify that I am an actor? Do I also have documents to certify that I am not an actor?

I am alone. I am helpless. No one is on my side. She has a group. Everyone is on her side. I have neither right nor chance to deny that I am an actor. She has either right or chance to prove that I am an actor. I feel very bitter to I find myself in this unpleasant situation. Maybe she had to take some months or years to plot this.

"You have not answered my question yet."

"What?"

"You seem to forget to answer my question."

"I think I already have."

She gives a light laugh.

I feel that her laugh is not real.

Then with a laugh, she says, "OK. Here is the question," then she asks slowly, "W h a t d r o v e y o u t o b e a n a c t o r?" She pronounces each word with unnecessary emphasis.

I don't like her tone of voice. I don't like her way of speaking with false intonation. It is like that of a short-tempered investigative police officer who questions a suspect angrily and impatiently. However, the expression on her face shows that she does not get short-tempered. Judging from the expression, she is in a good mood. Perhaps she seems to have a great ability to mask her emotion or perhaps she is really in good mood. Anyhow I am not ready to accept that everything I experience now is real. I have no confidence in her. Instead, I feel that she belongs to, or is indirectly related to, those who make me believe that I am an actor or who mistake me for the actor who is identical to me. From my mother I never heard that I had an identical twin brother.

By now I invent a story in my mind.

In a rainy day of July, in a temporary, shabby shack in a construction site, two identical twin brothers were born. Their teenage parents were construction laborers whose daily income could not afford to nourish and educate two children. They were uneducated. They were poor. They had no chance to dream, to go to middle school. At the age of twelve they started as construction laborers. They grew up together in construction sites. The shacks at the construction sites were their homes. They did not know what education was. They had no great hope. They had no knowledge about the importance of life. They got up in the morning and would work. And in the evening they would rest. At night they would sleep. Before they slept, they sometimes would make love. This was their daily routine. The day they worked was the day they had income. The day they did not work was the day they had no income. As laborers, they married young. They had no marriage certificate. They had no future plan. They did not really know for what they married.

As parents, they did not know what to do for their twin babies. But they knew well that their small and unsteady income could not afford to feed their two sons. They knew well they could not rely on their siblings or on their other relatives. When the babies were three months, the mother made a heartbreaking decision, as advised by a female senior engineer.

"My friend has no child," the engineer said. "She will adopt your son legally. You can trust her."

The mother was shocked. Then she cried. And the engineer tried to soothe her. The engineer had two daughters and a son. Her eldest daughter was in the tenth grade and her youngest daughter was in the third grade. Her son was in the sixth grade. She, as a mother, could sympathize with her feeling.

"I would like you to give an advice only. You can decide as you like," she explained. "You should ask yourself. You have an answer. I have nothing to say what it is right or wrong. Whatever you decide is right." The mother was in a dilemma.

This was how the twin brothers' life began. From then on they were separated.

I am one of the identical twins. If I remember rightly, I could try to get a so-called degree. As a victim of poor education system of our country, from so-called education, I got nothing but a degree. I studied English and Burmese. I read books on hand and became an avid reader. Later I came to realize that I had a talent in language and translation. This is why I started to translate. The story I translated first was *First Love* written by I.S Turgenev. I translated it, because I liked it much. Unfortunately, it was not published. Another famous translator translated it into Burmese. Some years later, I came across a copy of his Burmese translation in a bookshop. I don't remember the name of the publication house and the date of publication. But I remember its Burmese title.

I had no chance to meet my twin brother. I had no knowledge of my twin brother. I had no knowledge of his existence. My parents passed away six years ago. My mother died first; two years later, my father died. My parents took the secret with them. I never saw my identical twin brother. He also was adopted by a wealthy family, and is a famous actor now. I am mistaken for him.

My invented story is great! What are your views? Reasonable or unreasonable? Logical or illogical? Can you confirm that everything which has happened and happened to us is reasonable and logical? We all know that in the world such unreasonable stories have happened, happen and will happen.

Let the story be as it is. But where is my identical twin brother? Is he dead? Is he lost? Is he kidnapped?

And I feel that the others in the room might know what we are talking even though they can't hear us converse. Is it possible? No matter whether they know about what we are talking. When our conversation pauses for a while, the whole room goes silent as though there is no one in the room. Every object in the room remains silent. Everyone in the room is being busy with his or her own work or maybe everyone is pretending to be busy. Anyway, it is clear that no one pays attention to anyone. One neglects the other's presence and existence. There is no verbal or gestural communication among the people in the room. Everyone is alone. Everyone is detached. Our conversation is the only verbal and gestural communication in this room.

Everyone seems to be afraid that s/he might happen to do something wrong. Everyone seems to feel that everything and everyone is being recorded, photographed by CCTV cameras. Everyone seems to feel that everything and everyone is being watched by someone, using CCTV cameras. I look up at the ceiling. The ceiling is painted white. I don't see any CCTV cameras. The walls I see are painted light red. I have never seen the walls painted light red. Red is warm color. But light red here is not warm, very pleasant to see instead. I love it though I have no idea why they painted the walls light red. They may have a certain aim or symbol. Light red might be a lucky color for them. Or light red might be a healthy color for them. Or light red might be a warning for them. It could be that the walls are painted light red without any intention or any symbol. Light red, however, has a certain meaning or symbol for those who see it. Some years ago, I had a view that bulls hate red. And that is why bullfighters use red cape called *muleta* to excite the bull's anger. Later I read a short note that bulls, like other cattle, are color-blind to red: they can't discriminate between red and other colors. It only sees the movements. It is the movement of cape not color of the cape that can irritate the bull to charge. In other words, the cape, no matter what color, can irritate the bull with its movements. It was since the early 18th century that red capes started being used. In reality, red capes are used because they are considered an important part of the culture and tradition of bullfighting. From this we can see that red has to do with the audience, not with the bull. And the question is: why does red cape have to do with audience? Here we can see the words 'culture' and 'tradition'. It is obvious that the color is related to culture and tradition. OK. What is *culture*? What is *tradition*? Culture or tradition is surely associated with people in a certain society.

Red has ability to condition people. Red means *blessings* for the Chinese and *hell* to the ancient Egyptians. Why different people have different views on red? Is red responsible for this? Or are people responsible for this? Does red make people see it in different ways? Or do people make red have different meanings? Can we say that red is red? Can we say that red has no meaning, no symbol, no conditioning force to excite people?

On the walls, I don't see any CCTV cameras. But there, somewhere on the wall, hidden CCTV cameras might be planted, and somewhere in another room someone—I don't know who s/he is—might be watching everything and everyone every second, I think. We have no right to commit even a small mistake.

The question appears in my mind: is it necessary to watch us? To be watched is to lose a basic human right. I don't want to be watched like that. I want to do everything freely. The thought that there must be some hidden CCTV cameras and some hidden microphones somewhere in the room makes me feel rather out of sorts. The knowledge that I am being watched, that everything I say is being recorded, corners me. And I struggle to drive the thought away. Damn it! My attempt ends in vain. The thought is stranded in my mind.

By now I notice another young woman sitting across from me. She is in pink uniform. I can tell you that the pink uniform suits her. She has a slim body, fair complexion, bright, beautiful eyes and thin, red lips.

She is the second interviewer. She speaks clearly and confidently. Sometimes she pauses to choose her words carefully. She is sitting still, focusing her eyes on me, focusing her mind on what we are talking about. Surely she is interested only in what she is doing, not in anything else. Her face is serene, which signifies that her mind is balanced to a certain degree. It might be that she has practiced keeping her mind balanced. Without any practice, it is hard to keep the mind balanced. I must admit that I can't keep my mind balanced all the time. In my boyhood, I was very crabby. Parents did not want their children to play with me. And I always played alone. It was not a problem. I liked loneliness. I remember well that I beat a boy of my own age when I was young. I don't know the main reason why, I was a crabby boy. Was it because of the environment where I lived? My parents were very polite; especially my mother was very polite, pious and kindhearted. She always told me not to quarrel with anyone, not to fight with anyone. And whenever she heard that I fought with someone, she never hesitated to reprove me. I am awed by her, and I tried my best to be a good boy.

By now I am no longer crabby, I, however, try hard to show tolerance towards everything good or bad I experience and keep my mind balanced. Most of the time I fail, but I don't give up. I endeavor again and again. It seems that I begin to remember some parts of my real life now. It is a blessing, isn't it? And how about this situation? Can I show tolerance towards this predicament, too? Can I make my mind balanced while I am in this predicament?

One minute or one second ago, the second interviewer might be somewhere else in this room or outside. It could be that she entered the room a few minutes ago. If so, through which door did she enter the room? To my right, there are no doors nor windows. To my left there are no doors nor windows. The wall in front of me has neither doors nor windows. But I am not sure whether the wall to which I am sitting with my back has doors or windows. I, therefore, can say that she entered through it.

I am not sure where she has been, but I am sure she was not here in my presence; she was not here, in this room, sitting across like now. Maybe I overlooked her presence or maybe I have been too absorbed in my own thoughts that I couldn't spot her presence. Don't you think it is strange that I did not see her sitting still across from me a few minutes or a few hours ago? Don't you feel it is strange that I was not aware of her presence? I am not sure whether she has been here since the conversation started. I am not sure when the conversation started. Surely I am not blind. Surely I don't have bad eyesight. My eyesight does not fail at all. I can see everything clearly and vividly. If it is true, why didn't I spot her presence? I must say yes to the fact that I really was not aware of her presence. If she was my assassin, I would have been dead by now. I blame myself for my negligence. Can I rely on my eyesight any longer?

No. It is not true. Certainly I have good eyesight. I am neither near-sighted nor far-sighted. My eyesight does not fail. I do not wear spectacles. I can even see the eye of a small needle, and it is impossible that she could hide herself from me. She must have psychic powers to make herself invisible from me. Once I say like that in my mind, strangely some titles—*Invisible, The Invisible, The Invisible Man*—occur in my mind. I wonder why these titles come into my mind. Is it because those titles are partly related to me? Is it because I kept them in my memory once? If so, when did I store them in my memory? I have no idea how and when I stored them in my memory. At the moment, it is unclear to me even what they are. It seems that my memory does not work well enough to recognize those titles in detail.

While I am wrestling with the titles, she is wrestling with typing. The room is so silent that I can hear her touch the keys of her laptop now and then. She, like the first interviewer, is very good at typing, too. When I am about to ask her, some names appear in my mind. I ask myself why I remember these names and how these names are related to the titles. It will take time to be able to recognize everything. I always boast about how I have a good memory, but now I see that my memory does not work well enough: I can't recognize anything but titles and names. I am about to curse my memory.

I am fatigued and overwrought. Fucking memory.

"You should not blame your memory. Your memory is good. It seems that you have no knowledge about those titles and names. It seems that you did not put any data about those titles and names into your memory, and so you can't. Maybe from someone you learnt these titles and names. It seems that he told you nothing but titles and names."

Finally, I, with the help of something, manage to extricate myself from the crisis. No more stress. No more tension.

I don't want to upbraid myself any longer. Whether I overlooked or not, does not matter any longer. Everything already has happened without my awareness. What can I do? What I can do is to admit that I can't. I shake my head. I shrug my shoulders. I make myself prepared for what might happen to me next. I have no ability to know what will happen to him next, in a few seconds or in a few nanoseconds. My ability to know things is very limited. It seems that what I know is what I am allowed to know. I don't know what I am not allowed to know. And you? And the others?

I give the second interviewer a quick glance. She does not notice it. Or she seems to pretend not to notice it.

From her expression, I can guess that I am not familiar to her. But according to the data in my memory, she is familiar to me. I sense intimate relationship. Was she my high school friend? Was she my university friend? Maybe we became friends in primary school or in middle school, in high school or in college, or in university. I know nothing but that I know her. The important data in memory seems to be deleted or damaged.

"You have right to say: 'This is possible or this is impossible,' but you can't say: 'Let this be possible or let this be impossible.' Being possible or being impossible is beyond your power, beyond your knowledge," the second interviewer continues. "Your power is very limited. Your knowledge is very limited. You think that I was somewhere five minutes ago. No. I have been sitting here for three hours." She pauses for thought or for breath or for something.

I feel that her tone of voice seems to mock at me for I was unaware of her presence. If my ears did not cheat me, I really heard 'three hours'. Really has she been sitting here for so long? Is three hours' length of time long? No. Three hours' length of time is not long. Three hours' length of time is one-eighth length of time of a day. Therefore, three hours' length of time is not so long, compared to twenty-four hours' length of time. No. Three days' length of time is not so long, compared to three months' length of time. No. Three months' length of time is not so long, compared to three years' length of time. No. Sometimes even three minutes' length of time is so long, so unbearable. Three minutes' length of time is enough for destruction. It would not take more than three minutes for Paul Warfield Tibbetts Jr. to drop *Little Boy* on the city of Hiroshima or to drop *Fat Man* on the city of Nagasaki.

What does *three minutes before 08:15 on the morning of 6 August 1945* mean to Hiroshima? What does *three minutes after 08:15 on the morning of 6 August 1945* mean to Hiroshima?
What does *three minutes before 11:02 on the morning of 9 August 1945* mean to Nagasaki? What does *three minutes after 11: 02 on the morning of 9 August 1945* mean to Nagasaki?

And what do all these questions mean to you? Something or nothing or everything?
"I did not say, 'I have been sitting here for so long,' I said, 'I have been sitting here for three hours,' as you heard," she says. Her tone of voice is like the tone of voice of a teacher who explains a term or an expression to students. She seems to want me to understand what she really means or she seems to warn me not to misunderstand.
I remain mute. I wonder why she is explaining to me like that. Perhaps she has something special to say about time and space. I want to hear what she will say about time and space. It is a very interesting subject. We can't flee from time. We can't rebel against time. We are under control of time. Time to get up. Time to go to school. Time to go to bed. Time to take a rest. Time to go to work. Time to tear, time to amend. Time to speak. Time to be silent. Time to love. Time to hate. The word *time* is making a loud sound in my mind. Who did invent time?
We don't know who invented time or *time*. But we know who invented the first hourglass, a device for measuring time. It is said that in the 8th century AD a French monk called Liutprand invented it. Besides, we also learn that ancient Egyptians invented the *clepsydra* or water clock to measure the passage of

time. And it is said that hourglass represents the present as being between the past and the future and symbolizes time. Hourglass is the symbol of time, too. Even now, we lost a certain amount of sand from the top glass container.

Time is what we can't see. But *time* is what we can see.

It was in my mind that I was telling myself about three hours. In reality, I am not interested in the length of time. Really, I would like to ask her whether she is interested in the length of time and in time and space. I am not interested in time and space. In fact *time and space* is time and space. Your interest in, or your indifference to, *time and space* is nothing to time and space.

At first I did not know who and what she is. I thought I knew nothing but that she might be one of my friends. By now I come to realize that I was wrong. I recognize her. She is a short story writer. Surely, I know her as a short story writer. Among her peers, she is very bright, upbeat and ambitious. Though I can't recall her pen-name at present, I am sure that I like most of her short stories. Three years ago, she got the Reader Prize for her short story, the title of which I forgot but the plot and leading character of which I can remember well.

The story is about a young woman (She is named Miss Doubt, because she doubts everything) who is in a dilemma over whether to confess or to deny that she murdered her lover, by cutting his throat. She could not believe that it was her that committed such a cold-blooded crime, but in her mind, she saw herself killing her lover; she could not erase the crime scene. In her dreams she killed other men several times. Everyone she killed in her dreams was a man of about forty: her lover too was about forty. She was ten years younger than he was. She remembered in detail the scene of how she killed her lover. The scene did not frighten her at all. She enjoyed the scene very much. However, she thought that it was not she who killed her lover, it was someone else. She saw another young woman cutting her lover's throat in cold-blood. She was murmuring. She did not spot fear on her lover's face. He seemed to be experiencing the taste of having his throat cut open. From the expression on his face, she concluded that her lover enjoyed being cut.

She murmured, "Pain is good, isn't it?"

Her lover said nothing. He seemed to know beforehand that he would be killed like that. No surprise on his face. No sign of bitterness, no sign of shock on his face. But sign of tranquility, sign of peace on his face. Possibly he died in peace. He rested in peace.

Miss Doubt always spent time with her lover in a flat every weekend. Sometimes they had sex. Sometimes they spent time by telling things they've read or they've experienced or they've imagined. Both were book-lovers. Both were movie-lovers. Both liked freedom. So they did not want to tie one another with marriage. She was a free young woman, and he a free man. Both had no spouse. So they could spend their spare time in a flat together at any time they wanted.

It was at a wedding ceremony of her friend that she met him. She never hoped that she would fall in love with him. After she lost her boyfriend, she never thought that she would fall in love with another man. She had never slept with her boyfriend. They loved each other so much, and planned to marry when they got a degree. In final year, her boyfriend died suddenly, without any serious disease. Some thought that he died of food poisoning. Some thought that he committed suicide by taking poison. Some thought that he died of a disease which no one could identify. She was the last one who was with him, and suspicion fell on her. Fortunately, everyone kept their suspicion secret for some reason, and she was not inspected by the police. Fortunately, no postmortem was carried out. Anyway she sensed that she was being treated by his and her close friends with suspicion. She, therefore, left her home town four months later after the incident. It was six years later that she fell in love with the man who was her lover by now. She told him everything she did and everything she went through in the past.

"No matter whether you are responsible for the death of your boyfriend," he said. "I am not interested in what happened to you and what you did in the past. If we can live in the present together, it is OK."

She tried to avoid the thought that she was partly responsible for her boyfriend's death. When he came to say goodbye to her, she should have noticed that it would be the last time that they conversed. She remembered everything they two chatted that night. They talked and talked. They talked about their childhood.

They talked about how they fell in love with each other. The two of them never quarreled. The two of them were never angry with each other. She never sulked. And she could not imagine why he committed suicide. She did not think that he committed suicide or that he died of food poisoning. It might be that he was poisoned, she thought. Who did it? But she could not identify the culprit. As far as she could recall, he did not have any foe. He was very generous, affable, helpful, and sympathetic. So it is impossible that there was someone who wanted to kill him by poisoning. He was the only son: he was the sole heir to everything his parents owned. Therefore, there was no sibling who would murder him for inheritance. He had one uncle and two aunts from his mother's side, three aunts from his father's side. No suspicion fell on them. His uncle had no contact with his parents. His uncle, however, loved him very much. There was a connection between them. This was a secret for others, but not for her, but she knew everything about his uncle, because he told her everything about his uncle.

"Your uncle is a good man," she said.

"No one, including my mother, thinks like that," he said.

She noticed his tone of voice. Surely he felt sorry for his uncle.

His uncle took part in student movements and was arrested and imprisoned. He could not continue his education, because he could no longer commit anything to his memory. He could not remember words. He could not remember events. Sometimes he could not even remember who he was. He forgot even the fact that he was so much interested in literature. The fact he was a university student disappeared from his memory. He was an avid reader. The books he kept in his small home library will tell you what kind of reader he was.

At first she suspected the man. Later from her innate ability, she came to see that the man would not do such an inhuman thing. In this way the story about her boyfriend's sudden death evaporated. Even in her memory, the story about his death, the story about them, turned into a dream which she was not sure whether she really had or not.

I stop thinking about the short story in my memory for a while to ask myself how the whole plot of the story is imprinted in my memory in detail. No answer. I tell myself that it is impossible to get a certain answer to a certain question. Some questions have no answer, because they are questions without answers. Have I ever seen such type of young woman in my life, in my country? I am not certain. A name of a young woman comes into my mind. Did I have an affair with her? Does she really exist outside? Was she my girlfriend once? I can't visualize her. The name in my memory might be the name of a character in a work of fiction or in a novel written in Burmese. Before I can identify her, another name of a young woman comes into my mind. She is an educated young woman. It seems that I fell in love with her. But it is strange that I can't recall when and how the two of us met. It seems that we loved each other so much. The story about us in my memory is happy. Although I can't recall how it started and how it ended, I am sure that it is a good story with a happy ending. As far as I can recall, she is beautiful; she is bright; she is clever; she is well-bred; she is modest. My memory tells me that she is well-educated. She has a vast knowledge. How is this possible? I know well that our state's formal education can give us degrees, but can't educate us well. Instead it makes us mindless morons. So it is unbelievable that she is well-educated. It seems that she is a young woman free from our state education.

"The young woman in your memory is the young woman in a novelette written by a Burmese writer."

I hear the first interviewer say. I believe in what she says. When I realize I mistake the young woman in the novelette for the young woman in my imagination, my heart sinks. I see that I don't want to accept reality. I, however, don't want the young woman in my imagination to be a phantom. I want her to be real. Everything I keep in my memory of her is different from reality. What a fucking good memory!

I look at the first interviewer to say thank. She is reading what she has typed on her laptop screen. It seems that she said nothing; instead, she is obsessing over what she has written. If so, who said it? The second interviewer? I don't think so. The second interviewer is being in deep thoughts. She likes it. She has a habit of living alone with her own thoughts. She only has a few friends. When she was a child, she did not play with the other girls. She did not even play with her siblings. She loves loneliness. She loves solitude. She had been a very taciturn girl.

It is unbelievable that such a girl becomes an interviewer. I wonder what changed her habitual pattern of mind. For me it is hard to believe that she is an interviewer. I tell myself in my mind that she is just acting. I stop thinking about who said it.

Now my thoughts go back to the prize-winning story.

It was a rainy day. At about twelve, she phoned her lover to come to the flat they always spent time in together. They talked about the movies they watched. Coincidentally, both loved movies, especially, they liked the mystery movies such as *The Conversation, Gone Girl, Inception, Shutter Island, Seven, Identity* etc. Strangely, most of the movies they've watched were the same. They wondered why they both liked the same type of movies. Whenever they were together they shared views on the movies they had watched. When they met, for the last time, they talked about the film they would like to make.

"It is impossible to know everything," he said. "Human knowledge is limited. We know what we are allowed to know. We don't know what we are not allowed to know."

She laughed heartily and said, "You are a philosopher."

"Why?"

"Kant also said: *Human knowledge is limited*. And now you say the same thing."

Her lover shrugged his shoulders. He was not interested in philosophy; he was lazy to think. He liked not thinking. When he was twenty or so, he and his friends always mocked their fellow university students of philosophy. At the time they were not familiar with this: 'Philosopher is a blind man in a dark room looking for a black cat that is not there.' He wanted to lead an easy life. He was not ambitious. He was not studious. Strangely, he never failed his examinations. No one imagined that such an indolent student would get a masters' degree. Among his relatives, he being the first person who got a masters' degree, his parents were so proud of his success. However, he did not think that it was his success. He felt nothing for getting a masters' degree. He knew well that his masters was nothing but a name.

He was born to a considerably rich family as the youngest son, so no need to worry for him to earn money. His parents were successful brokers of agricultural products. His parents, his elder brothers and elder sisters were born in the country, but he was born three years later after his parents moved to a small town. In his family, he was the only one who was introduced to the urban life once after birth. Only when he was ten, he paid a first visit to his parents' native village, with his older siblings. He liked the country life style. He felt free there in the village. But he never dreamt to dwell in the village, because he became bored when one month passed in the village.

He fell in love with a beautiful village girl, who was three years older than him. It was the first time he ever kissed a girl's lips and cheek. Some years later, he forgot her name, yet he never forgot his first experience of kissing. No one knew that they fell in love with each other. Perhaps the two were too good at keeping it a secret or perhaps the others pretended not to know it. When summer holidays were over, they left the village. When he said goodbye, his girl wept, but he did not. He knew well that his heart sank.

Though he could not recall her name, her face and figure were imprinted in his memory forever. Her gentle voice was still in his ears. Her lovely gesture he could see. She had a slim body and a fair complexion. She had wide eyes and thick eye-brows. She had a pretty face and a straight nose. Her short, blond, curly hair made her different from the other village girls. The village girl was his first love and Miss Doubt was his second love.

Miss Doubt, when she heard the news of her lover's death, felt horrified. She had no idea why she felt like that. However, when she witnessed the crime scene, she witnessed she was calm, not shocked or terrified. Though the news of her lover's death horrified her, the crime scene of her lover could not terrify her. What a strange thing! She could not imagine why she felt like that.

Did she really kill her lover? She was sure that she never committed such a crime. She was not prepared to confess that she committed the crime. She was prepared to receive the punishment which she thought she deserved. All evidences proved that she had murdered. But no one tried to find those evidences. No one suspected her. No police officer came to her. Everything was as usual. She felt surprised: all newspapers and journals reported that her lover died of heart failure. She did not believe in what she read, but the photos of her lover in the newspapers showed that it was true. She saw no wound on her lover's throat. He was lying on his back, with half-opened eyes.

She saw a faint smile on his face. She knew well that it was a satisfactory smile. Surely he faced death with ease. Surely he felt at ease on his deathbed.

What is real? she asked herself. She could not believe what she experienced. She thought that something must be wrong and she could not find out what was wrong.

No doubt that if one was true, the other would be false. If the fact that he died of heart failure was true, the fact that he died of the knife wound would be false. If the fact that he died of the knife wound was true, then the fact that he died of heart failure would be false. She doubted whether she cut his throat with a knife; possibly it was just in a dream that she did it. In fact, she should be happy for she really did not kill her lover. But she was not happy now. Why? Was it because she wanted to be sentenced to death or to be imprisoned for years as a murderer? She had no reason to kill him. She did not hate him. There were no problems between them. It was true that they had different views. Having different views is not a problem. It is just nature. They two never quarreled over this issue. They did not try to understand each other; they understood each other: not because she was meek, but because he was meek.

Did he really die? Did he pretend to die? Impossible. Any newspaper or any journal would not print his death if he really did not die. She failed to attend his funeral. On the day when his funeral was held, she was on a journey. She set on a journey the day before his funeral. By now she thought that she should attend his funeral to be sure how he died.

Five months later, she came back from her journey. No one talked about his death any longer. Almost everyone forgot him. It was as if he did not really live on this earth. He was a phantom, which was removed by now from the minds of his friends, of his fellows, of his relatives.

Miss Doubt stayed five months in a small town to keep herself away from what she had done. One day she was sipping her coffee, sitting at table in the corner (she always sat in the corner) of a coffee bar, when a girl of about eighteen entered. The bar was not crowded. There were three empty tables, but she did not walk to those tables; she walked straight to the two-person table at which Miss Doubt was sitting, and asked permission to sit. She said yes. The girl sat opposite her. A waitress came to her and handed the menu to the girl. Without looking at the menu, she ordered Americano to the waitress. Miss Doubt noticed that the girl was after her own heart. A few minutes later, the waitress brought her a coffee cup, a small packet of sugar, a small cup of milk, and a small spoon.

Miss Doubt watched everything. The girl tore the small packet of sugar, poured it into the coffee cup first, then she took the cup of milk and poured some into the coffee cup, and then she stirred it with the small spoon. Then she lifted the cup and tasted the coffee. A satisfactory expression appeared on her face. After she had sipped two or three times, she put the cup down and pulled a book from her backpack. She opened the book and started to read it; she seemed to be a bookworm. A few minutes later she was deep in the book.

Miss Doubt saw the book cover, and knew that it was a novel that she had read two years ago. She read it from cover to cover more than six times, and knew the whole novel by heart. It was her lover who bought a copy of the book to her on her birthday. Majority of readers did not like it, but she liked it inordinately. When she talked to her friends about the novel, she noticed sudden a change of expression on their faces. From their expression, she could tell that the novel horrified them.

Obviously, they never had read such a horrifying novel.

She was about to say that she had already read the book more than six times, but she feared that the girl would be annoyed by her words and so, she kept herself silent.

The silence between the girl and Miss Doubt prolonged. She had no idea how to break the silence. She, therefore, remained silent.

This is just a small part of the story. I can tell you the whole story in detail. I can't imagine how the plot of her short story remains stuck in my memory. You can't tell a story in detail if it is not written by you. That is why I doubt that it is the story written by her. Maybe I mistake my story for hers. If so, I must be a writer. I am sure I am not a writer. I am a translator.

"May I know why you tried to commit suicide?" she asks, looking straight at me. The camera operator in white T-shirt shoots the close-up of the woman's face while she asks me that question. The other camera closes in on me.

The question pounds my head hard. I am sure that I never committed suicide. Even the slightest thought to kill myself has never occurred to me. I don't mean that I always enjoy my life, I am always happy. Sometimes I felt tired of life. I, however, never thought I would end my life. I don't think that suicide is the right way of solving problem. I never thought to curse the day I was born. I accept the view that life is very precious, living is very valuable. Living is better than dying, isn't it?

One of my friends committed suicide. No one knew what kind of problems he had. He was very honest. He left high school and became a night watcher at the high school he attended as a student. He did not have many friends. Maybe it was because he was aloof. I paid a visit to my native town four months before his death. I did not know that it would be the last time I had a talk with him. We spent some hours reminiscing about our boyhood and about the dreams in our boyhood. I did not see any sign in the expressions on his face that he would commit suicide four months later. I did not see any sign of depression on his face for the failure of his boyhood dreams. His eyes were bright with happiness.

In my view life is to live. I must confess that sometimes I feel tired of life. You should not take this as the idea to commit suicide. It is a just a turning point.

"Why do you ask this question?" I ask her. I try to manage my tone of voice, but I know that my tone of voice can't cover my resent. Her question is not an insult, but it annoys me.

She does not answer my question. She asks me another question instead. I must have misheard her.

"Have you ever starred as a translator before?"

"No. This is the first time."

"And you have some problems with acting, haven't you?"

"Not so many."

"Not so many?"

"Of course, not so many."

"Oh, great! And did you study how translators lead their lives?"

"I am sorry. I am not sure whether I did so," I say. "But I am sure I am familiar with how translators lead their lives. But please don't ask me why. I have no answer."

Translators in our country lead hard lives. Any book of translation does not sell more than one thousand copies. They get ten or fifteen percent of the book's price. It takes three or four months to translate a book. Their income is very small: it is impossible for a translator to live on translation alone. He must have other jobs, as well. The result is that a translator can't keep on translating.

This is the film about a translator. The main character in this film has to lead a hard life, too. He is about thirty-five years old. He has translated six books of fictions. Four of them have been published. The book he translated first was a novel written by an American novelist John Irving. While translating *The Cider House Rules*, he worried that the publisher would not appreciate the book. When the publisher gave him the green light, he rejoiced. He is a self-taught translator. He reads everything on hand.

Maybe this is the synopsis-like thing of the film. I can't imagine why this synopsis-like thing is in my mind.

Did I read the synopsis or the entire script for the film?

Why did I read the synopsis or the script if I am not an actor?

Why do these thoughts occur to me if I am sure that I am not an actor?

Does this imply that I sense that I am unsure?

I am being haunted by questions.

Chapter III
Of My Mind

I am here, sitting in the bleak room. The beautiful, self-possessed young woman in the red uniform is asking me questions. At the same time, I am there, sitting on the flat ground of Great Pagoda Hill of my native town. My best friend in white shirt is telling me stories from his mind. My friend is a good story-teller. We are tenth standard students. This afternoon the two of us play truant.

"It is about a boy," my friend starts another story. "He is poor, but bright. That is why the villagers dub him Bright Boy. He likes his new name. In reality, he is bright; he learns anything quickly. He has an excellent memory. He can even recall things that the others have forgotten. He is very kind-hearted. He always helps others. He never does bad deeds. He never hurts others."

"The boy is very perfect."

"Yes, he is."

"I have never met such a perfect boy," I comment.

I know well that he also has never met such a perfect boy.

Then he continues telling his fable-like story. He is always earnest when telling such stories. Sometimes he shows me what he has written. His writing is good. It is incredible that a high school student can write so well. However, he has never entered the essay competition in our school. The odd thing was that I did not enter the essay competition at our school, because I was very bad at writing. But oddly he did not, because he, unlike me, is good at writing. He never told me why not. And I never asked him why not. He is a talkative boy while he has a story to tell me. But he is a silent boy when he has no story to tell me or he has no will to tell me any story. He dwells in his thoughts as if he is alone.

"The boy wanted to help his poor villagers," he says. "And he always tried to find out the way to help his villagers. He spent most of his time, thinking about how he will able to help his poor villagers. He had a firm belief in that he would be able to help his villagers one day. He, however, did not know how."

"How can a poor boy help other people?" I ask.

He smiles. "He can," he replies, "because he has great will to help other people. What we need is such a great will."

I shake my head. "Your story is like a fable," I interrupt.

"Exactly. It is a fable or fable-like story, like that of Kafka."

"Who is Kafka?"

"A German-language writer."

"He was a German?"

"No. He was Jew. I have told you about him several times. Did you forget?"

I shrug my shoulders.

"Oh, terribly sorry. You know. I am not as bright as you are. I have a poor memory."

He sighs as if feeling disappointed. His eyes reveal that he is not disappointed. He knows well that I have a very bad memory, but he has never blamed me for it. Sometimes he gave me good techniques to make memory good. I never tried.

"You do not remember what I told you about Kafka. Anyway you know that my story is fable-like."

"Of course, I do."

"Why?"

"Sorry, I have no idea."

"You don't know the reason. Do you?"

"No, I don't."

His expression changes. Whenever he starts to say something serious, his expression always changes.

"Whether you know or not, there is a reason."

"Is there a certain reason why I know that your story is fable-like?"

His face shines. "Surely, there is. The reason is your knowledge."

"My knowledge?"

"Yes, what you have learnt or what you have been taught."

"I can't follow," I say.

"Think hard," he says.

Then we laugh. When he stops laughing he says seriously, "A small thing in my story put a question into your mind finally. That, is the point."

"What?" I can't get what he means. When I look at him, I see a mysterious expression on his face.

"OK, let me ask you a question." he says.

I gesture him to ask me the question.

"Why do you think that my story is fable-like?"

"I have answered you."

"I know. Please try another one."

I think, and think and think. Then I answer, "I feel that your story is illogical, because…"

"That is enough," he interrupts before I finish my sentence. "That is the point. This shows that you can't accept something unreasonable and illogical. In other words, your rationality warns you not to accept what is unreasonable or illogical. Fables are beyond rationality," he pauses to choose the right words.

I shrug my shoulders. I have nothing to argue. I am not a good thinker like him. I am not a good speaker like him.

"You have been taught directly or indirectly, knowingly or unknowingly, willingly or unwillingly not to believe easily in what is beyond your ability to reason," he pauses and studies me, as a scientist studies an object. "My story is illogical," he says, "because I want it to be illogical. I admit. But as you know, sometimes things happen illogically."

I nod and parrot his words: "Sometimes things happen illogically."

"Here we use the word 'illogically', because it is beyond our reasoning power," he explains.

He is right. Sometimes things happen illogically. Reasoning is the wrong code for the thing which is beyond reason. Sometimes what really happens to us is totally different from what we can really reason. Events in the history prove that this theory is true. In Burmese modern history, we learn about thirty comrades. No one knew beforehand or could not reason that one of the thirty comrades would become a cruel dictator and would ruin the whole Burma, fourteen years after its independence.

It is said that the would-be dictator was not among the would-be thirty comrades, who would take the last ship leaving for Hainan Island on 27th March, 1941. He was substituted for the other Thakhin (Thakhin is a Burmese word, meaning 'Master' or 'Sir' in English. This word has a long, interesting story. The one who coined this word is Ba Thaung. He was the one who started to put 'Thakhin' before his name. And he was known as Thakhin Ba Thaung. It meant Sir Ba Thaung or Master Ba Thaung in English.), who was chosen as a member of thirty comrades but could not come due to his sudden severe illness. It was in this way that he became one of the thirty comrades.

Later he became one of the worst dictators in the world. He imprisoned everyone whom he thought to be a threat to his power. He did not spare even the members of the thirty comrades and their family members. What led him to do this?

Bogyoke Aung San decided to appoint Thakhin Bahane as the Chief of the Staff of the Armed Forces, yet Thakhin Than Tun did not agree. The result was that the would-be dictator became the Chief of the Staff of the Armed Forces.

While he was the Chief of the Staff of the Armed Forces, some advised the prime minister of AFPFL (Anti-Fascist People's Freedom League) to fire him for several reasons, but the prime minister did not listen to their advice. A few military officers tried to assassinate him, but failed. Any attempt of assassination failed.

What kind of SPIRIT or THING did persuade Thakhin Than Tun to say no to Bogyoke's decision? What kind of supernatural BEING or THING did make the prime minister refuse the advice of the others? What kind of invisible supernatural FORCE did make the assassination attempt fail? Was it a god or God? No. I don't think so. If so, what and who was it? David was anointed by God to defeat a giant warrior, Goliath of Gath. By what was he anointed to turn our country into the abyss of poverty and illiteracy? In Burmese modern history, March 2nd, 1962 means something horrible. It means the end of parliamentary democracy. It means the damage of economy. It means fall of education. Our country was popular among countries of Southeast Asia then. But it ruined the popularity. Our country was famous for its educational system among the countries of Southeast Asia. Incredibly, it turned this fame and prestige of our nation upside-down. Our nation lost everything good and got everything bad.

Nothing can erase or conceal this inglorious episode in our history. This inglorious episode in our history will always haunt us. How did this happen to our nation? Who let the dictator do this? Surely I don't know. We don't know. You don't know. Sometimes our limited ability to know things hurts us.

Don't you think it is mysterious that I know Burmese modern history and her main characters? Am I a historian? Was I a history student? Am I studying Burmese history? Anyway it is certain that I am so much interested in history. To me history is a huge novel about what was really done by real people and what really happened to real humans in a certain past. Reading history gives me pleasure and things for contemplation. In truth, the history we are taught in our school is just a false history, which is written by frightened scholars. Therefore, we lost the precious chance to be familiar with the real history of our country. What we really learnt from school differs from what really happened. Hence it can be concluded that I did not earned this knowledge from our school textbooks. It was my history teacher who shared with me the knowledge of history. Majority of books which presented reality were banned during the reign of BSPP, because they could affect its power. My history teacher was a good speaker. He seemed to have forgotten to tell me that some real events are fable-like and illogical.

"And one day the boy had to clean the store room of the monastery in his village. There in the store room, he found a huge box."

My friend's words take me back from my wayward thoughts. I am not in thoughts about history, which is like a fable. I am now with my friend and with his story.

Before my friend starts saying another sentence, I signal him to pause.

"Something wrong?" he asks.

"No. Something missing," I correct.

"OK, go ahead."

"Your poor boy had to clean the store room of the monastery in his village."

I pause and check him.

"Yes, he had to," he replies.

And I add, "And he found a huge box in the store room."

"Of course, he found it there."

"And my question is: Was he the first one who had to clean the store room?"

My friend's eyes twinkle with the pleasure of realization of something.

"Oh, I see," he bursts out.

"You are a very bright guy. So I know that you will see this. If your poor boy was not the first one who had to clean the store room, the first boy who had to clean the room must had seen the box. OK? Don't you feel that something is lacking?"

"Cool!" he exclaims. Then he returns to his story. "He was not the first boy who had to clean the room. He was not sure who did clean the room first. He was not sure how many people and how many times the room had been cleaned before. He, however, was sure that he was the first boy who noticed the box. Here you can ask why the boy was sure that he was the first boy who noticed the box. Simple. It was because he was the first boy who noticed the box. He wondered why the other guys who cleaned the room did not notice the box. Was it because the box invisible to them? Or was it because something made them blind for a short moment when they were near the box? There were many possibilities.

"He was not a curious boy. He never tried to know anything he should not know. He was not a disobedient boy. He always obeyed every code of conduct. He never touched anything without knowledge of its owner. He never committed even a small immoral act. But now he was aware of his intense curiosity to see what was being kept in the box. He tried to suppress his temptation to open the box and see the stuff in it as far as he could, yet he failed. Something inside, or outside, his mind and body seemed to be so powerful that he went under control of it.

"He opened it on impulse. Unconsciously, his eyes fell on something in the box. It seemed that a certain spirit commanded him to take it. He could not resist the order. And he did as ordered. It was impossible for him to rebel against something powerful. He held the thing in his hand. He did not know what it was. He did not know that it was called a *scroll*, because he had never seen a scroll, because he had never heard the word *scroll*."

"But you know the word *scroll*."

"Yeah, I do."
"And have you ever seen the scroll?"
"Of course, I have."
"That is why you use this word in your story. Right?"
My friend nods, yet says nothing.

My friend was born in a small village. It is about nine hours' drive from our small town. His family moved to our small town when he passed the fourth standard. In his village, there was no middle school. He would have to walk to another big village where there was a middle school. There is a creek between his village and the other village. The students have to cross the brook to go to school. In the rainy season, it is very dangerous to cross the creek. Finally, his parents decided to move to town. They bought a house near ours. In this way the two of us became neighbors, friends and school mates. He has lived in the village for nearly nine years, he has vast knowledge about the village. And maybe it is in the monastery in his village that he saw the scroll. I don't ask him about the scroll he saw. What was written on the scroll he saw? Surely it might be interesting. But I am not a very curious boy like he is, so I can suppress my curiosity easily. I have never seen the scroll. The elders told me about some scrolls. Ancient Buddhist monks wrote Buddhist teachings on scrolls. What's more some ancient scholars recorded their ideas by writing on scrolls as well. So scrolls played a very important role in the ancient tradition of Burmese literature.

"He saw some patterns with grids, letters, words and numbers. He did not know what the words meant. He did not understand what the numbers referred to. The words and numbers cannot be said to have no meanings and qualities because he did not know their meanings. Though he had no idea of what they meant, they surely bore their own meanings and qualities. Anyway, it is sure that every letter, every word, every number and every line captivated him so much that he could not help scanning them. The more he scanned them, the more he was captivated by them. Maybe it was because something powerful was manipulating his mind and body."

"What is something powerful?" I ask.

He gives a hearty laugh. "Something powerful is something powerful."

"There might be no answer which is better than this one," I remark.

My friend shrugs his shoulders. "His eyes fell on a pattern with some simple grids and numbers, yet he did not know what it was."

"A pattern with some grids and numbers. What is that?" I ask.

He looks at me with surprised. "Don't you know what it is?"

"No. I don't," I reply. "Really, I don't know what it is."

"Have you never seen such thing before?"

"Never," I give a short answer.

"That is the point. From me you have heard the phrase, 'a pattern with some simple grids and numbers,' but you don't know what it is. It is simply because this is the first time you heard this. It is simply because you have no knowledge about this. In other words, there is no data about such a thing in your memory. It is certain that you did not put any data about this into your memory."

I am silent, not because I have nothing to say, but because I have many things to say. I am choosing the right words to speak.

I try to analyze the phrase, 'a pattern with some simple grids and numbers.' Surely I am familiar with each word. I know the word 'pattern'. I know the word 'grid'. I know the word 'number'. But I don't know what the phrase means. To be familiar with the words in this phrase is one thing and to know what the phrase means is another thing.

"The boy, like you, had no knowledge about this: it was the first time he was seeing it," my friend says.

"You don't want to let the boy have knowledge about that, do you?" I ask.

"No need to know what it is," he replies.

His reply is not the answer to my question. I shrug my shoulders. "You don't let the boy know what it was. Similarly, you don't let me know what it is."

"No, I don't."

"Don't you think it is unfair, do you?"

"I am the writer of this story. So I have the right to do whatever I want in my story."

"You mean you are the God of your story, don't you?"

"Sometimes I am. Sometimes I am not."

A brief silence.

"The boy tried to commit the pattern to memory, without knowing that the ogre warding it would help him with miraculous powers. He had an excellent memory, so it was not hard for him to memorize the pattern. He tried to draw the pattern in his mind several times until he was sure that he would be to draw it by heart."

"You used the word 'ogre'."

"Yeah, I did."

"Why didn't you use the word 'genie'?"

"I don't know why. But I feel that the word 'ogre' is more suitable in my story."

"OK, let it be. And may I know whether your ogre is like the genie in the fable 'Aladdin and the Wonderful Lamp'?"

He shakes his head. Then he frowns. And then he says thoughtfully, "I am sorry. It is very early to say that."

"Very early?"

He nods.

There is a long silence. He is gazing towards somewhere. I can swear that he is thinking about his story. His story is just beginning. He must tell how the pattern works, how the ogre appears. Though the boy has committed the pattern to mind, he has no idea about when he should draw it and on what should he must draw it. He is not even sure whether it is dangerous or helpful. There must be a certain hidden cause behind his finding the pattern. It might be a well-designed plan. The problem is that he does not know what kind of plan it is. Good or bad. Destructive or productive. He must activate the pattern by drawing it on something first.

A long silence. I love it. I think that sometimes we need silence, because sometimes silence brings us different types of excellent ideas. Now both of us are silent. Now we are both sitting without saying anything. He goes on writing his unfinished story in his mind. So he needs silence. I am not writing anything in my mind. But I also need silence, because I love silence. This place is silent. That is why I like this place. From this place I can get freedom from the urban noise. This means that I am free from urban noise or urban noise can't torture my ears and mind. Besides, it is pleasant to gaze at the scene of my little town from here. I come here for freedom from the urban noise only, and my friend comes here not only for freedom from the urban noise but for thoughts and imagination. The fresh air here refreshes us, and the touch of breeze drives worries and anxiety out of our minds. I don't know how meters high this hill is. I know that this place is high enough to see things clearly from above. No roof, no wall here. That is the other reason that I love this place. (This is all I can tell you about this place. This is all you can experience through the words. For you to have direct experience of this place, you will have to come here.)

We see other people here and there. Some are having a hearty conversation. Some are sitting still, deep in thoughts. I don't know what they are thinking. I am not the one who can see the thoughts in others' minds. I have heard about those who, with their psychic power, can read the others' minds. Two or three years ago I had a crazy idea to have such a power, because I wanted to know what other people were thinking. Later, I abandoned my idea.

My friend has probing eyes, good memory and great power of observation. All these qualities are those that I lack. I, however, never coveted such things. And so you may take me an idiot. He is lanky. I am not short, yet he is nearly four inches taller than I am. He seems to be older than he really is. It might be because he always buries himself in serious thoughts, I think. But I am not sure.

While I am waiting for the other parts of his story, my mind flies towards the past. And now I am a middle school student.

"What do you want to be?" my female teacher (Female teacher is called *Sayarma* in Burmese. And Burmese students address their female teacher *Sayarma*) asks me.

The answer is ready. For me no need to think about my aim two times. And I answer easily and quickly. I am surprised when the other students laugh at my simple answer. I have no idea why they laugh. My answer is simple. My answer is succinct. My answer is serious. My answer has no humor.

"Nothing, Sayarma."

I am standing straight in front of my teacher, holding my hands, in a brave manner of self-confidence. Their laughter can't move me even a little. To me my answer is great. I hope my teacher will be proud of me for my great answer.

To me my answer is sensible and meaningful, but to them my answer may be silly and ridiculous. Anyway, I am not mad at them. It is not because I am a very patient person but because I don't see their response as an insult. Besides, I realize that my demeanor might be strange to them. This does not mean that I don't know that they should not laugh at my word.

The roar fills the classroom. Only when the teacher beats the blackboard with a cane stick in her hand as the sign of warning, laughing stops. Their response to my word can do nothing to me. I think that maybe they are wondering what on earth am I doing. To their eyes, I might be an abnormal creature or an alien. But I feel neither ashamed nor embarrassed. I feel neither depressed nor inferior. But I cannot help asking myself why they don't accept the fact that a person can live without any idea of his future plan.

In their turns, they give different answers. Their answers are simple and easy. Some answer that they want to be engineers. Some answer that they want to be doctors. Some answer that they want to be military officers. I have no idea why they have such things in their minds. Who would put such funny things into their minds? We are all in sixth standard. Why do sixth standard students have such ideas?

Though everyone laughs at my answer, a student remains silent. It is Good Boy. I see him give me thumbs up: he likes my answer.

"Bravo! You are really great," praises Good Boy on the way to our homes.

I shrugged my right shoulder, and smiled.

"I am great. Why?"

"You have courage to divulge your idea," he remarked. "It is a challenging job. Now you have done it. Congratulation!"

I don't doubt his words. I sense that he is not flattering me.

"Very simple. I just told the truth," I replied. "I have no idea of what I want to be. And I don't want to say that I want to be a doctor or an engineer, because I don't want to be a doctor or an engineer. That is all."

"I see," he says. "To tell something true or to tell something false is not easy. Both demand courage."

"Both demand courage," I say, echoing his words.

He is right. However, when I declared my idea in class, it was not necessary for me to summon any courage. I did it simply. And I ask myself why people need courage to tell the truth in their hearts.

"Your answer was also good," I say.

He shakes his head. "In fact it is not what I want to answer."

"Your real answer is something else."

He nods.

"What is your real answer?" I ask.

"As you know, I always observe things and people, because I have interest in things and people. Then in my mind, I make stories. So what can be my real answer? Guess it."

"Wow, I see!" I exclaim. Then I comment, "So you lied the teacher."

"No, I did not."

"You did. You did not tell her your real aim."

"It is not my aim. It is what I want to do."

"Okay, you could tell the teacher about what you want to do."

"You are wrong. The teacher wants to know what I want *to be* not *to do*. They are different."

I stop arguing, because I know well that I can't argue with him. I am not a good speaker like him.

A few second later I make a comment, "Your real answer can be ridiculous to her."

"Surely, what she hopes is something else," he shrugs his shoulders.

"Something else?"

He does not give any answer to my question. And I try to find an answer to my question. Something good is too formal. The word 'good' cannot be put in a fixed definition. That is why 'something good' has no exact meaning.

In reality we have never seen a writer. In our small town, there are no accomplished writers who can inspire him to write. He wants to write stories without anyone to inspire him to do so. Why? Perhaps it is his basic instinct that inspires him to write. This is the easiest answer.

I have no dream for my future. However, my parents have special dreams for future. My father is a carpenter and my mother, a hawker: their income is so small and so unstable that they cannot afford to buy me even a bicycle. And I have to walk to the school. I must confess that I envy the other students who bike to school. In fact, I am not the only student who has to walk to school. There are other students, including my friend, Good Boy. I must admit that I am not a dutiful, clever son, but I am sure I understand my parents well. I never let them know that I want a bike. I don't want them to feel sad that they cannot buy me a bike.

As I've said, my parents have special dreams for my future. They both don't have a good education. But they want me to be educated. In reality they do not know what a real education is. The education they know is having a well-paid job and rank which can impress other people. They want me to be a teacher or an engineer or an army officer.

I am not sure what I will be in the future. I have no prescient wisdom. I have no idea of what I want to be. I am not ambitious. I am not interested in teaching. To me teaching is very boring. I know what an engineer is, because I find engineers in the construction site where my father works. Their job is to guide the workers like my father. I always see them being busy with a file in which some sheets of papers are kept. Sometimes they opened their files to order the workers what to do. And I asked my father why the engineers always open their like that.

"They are young engineers. They do not have enough experience."

I was not satisfied with my father's answer.

"Anyway, you should try to be an engineer."

"Why, Dad?"

"Because an engineer is superior to a worker, like me."

My father's answer was so simple that it was imprinted in my mind. I didn't tell my father that I did not want to be an engineer because I did not want him to be disappointed.

I am not a bright student. I am not good at sport. I am not good at mathematics or geometric. I am not good at writing composition. What I am good at is that I knew that I am not good at anything. I have neither skill nor ability which can impress others. It is not surprising that I am not one of the outstanding students of our school. Sometimes I happened to ask myself why I was born as such a stupid guy. Good Boy always counsels me that I should have certain ability. The problem is that I do not know what it is. He assured that one day I myself will come to see this ability. I am not sure whether his word is right or wrong. I am sure that his word consoled me much.

In contrast to me, my counselor was born with a brilliant mind and memory. He had good ideas. He had a skill at writing. He could try to be the best in our school, but he never tried. He was good at writing. Yet he never wrote a good composition. He could try to impress the other students. He never tried. When I asked him why, his answer is simple: "I don't want to be the best."

I imagined what it is like to be the best, yet I failed. Even now I can't imagine what is it really is.

We both have our own problems in life. Anyway, we are lucky enough to go to school. I have even seen some boys of my own age working as day-hired laborers. They are not lucky enough like us to go to school. What made them day-hired workers? The easy and visible cause is; poverty. And what is the invisible cause?

"The boy succeeds in activating the pattern," my story-teller friend restarts his fable-like story.

My thoughts come back from the middle school days, and I make myself ready to listen to his story.

Can I believe everyone in this bleak room? I feel unsafe. I feel that I am being watched by my foes. I want to confide in someone everything I undergo now. But I have no confidant and confidante. I don't have an intimate friend who will help me, who will advise me, who will save me. So I must save to myself. I myself try to escape from this room, from these people, and from this mess. It is hard to figure out what will happen to me next. Everyone is like robots, but not like aggressive robots. No sign of enmity in their expression. They are just working their works, without saying anything. Is even saying nothing dangerous? And I can do nothing but wait and see. Can the situation be worse than now?

You can say that they are not my enemies, they are just my colleagues. They are the ones who work together with me on a movie. The problem is that I don't know them. However, I feel that I know a young camera operator well. She is a young woman with red hair. She is about twenty-four. She is a poet, whose poems I like, I guess.

"May I know your name?" I ask.

She hesitates to tell me her name. She finds it hard to decide whether she should tell or not. She looks at the first interviewer, who nods towards her.

She tells me her name.

It is the name of a female experimental poet I have guessed she might be. I am satisfied to know that what I have guessed is correct.

"I have read all of your poems, and I like them all," I say, with the hope that she will be happy to hear her reader's praise. I am not flattering her. I really like her poems.

"Sorry, I am not the one you think," she explains. "I am not a poet." She seems to be annoyed. The expression on her face shows that she fears something and that she is in a tense mood. She adds, "I read poems, and especially I am interested in experimental poetry, but I have never tried to write a poem, because I know that I can't."

I repent to insist that she is the poet. It seems that my words reveal her secret. Do my words threaten her security? I swear that I didn't mean to put her in trouble.

I don't understand why she conceals her real identity.

The young woman asks me some questions about some foreign films I like. Strangely, some foreign movies enter my mind. Strangely, I find myself analyzing a foreign movie. She listens to everything I say, and writes down notes on her laptop. Why do I have such good knowledge about the movies? Maybe it is because I am a movie lover. This answer is not perfectly satisfactory. The way I analyze the movie shows that I am more than a movie lover. It suggests that I am a film director or an actor or a film analyst.

"Do you think your analytical knowledge in film is helpful for your acting?" she asks.

I think I say yes. And I can't imagine why I say so.

"Okay, now it is time to talk about your experience as an actor," she says.

The phrase 'it is time to' reminds me something to do. In my mind's eye, I see a young woman (I dub her Miss Moon, because she has a round, pretty face.) in bluff blouse. She is waiting for someone in the City Park. I feel that she is my lover, who teaches English at a college in a remote town. And I am the one whom she is waiting for. Last night, on the phone, she told me to have a chat over coffee in the evening. And the two of us made an appointment to meet in the City Park. She is ten years younger than I am. She is more patient than I am. She is more generous than I am. She is a bookworm. She, especially, loves mystery novels.

Last week, I picked her up at the railway station. She came to the capital to attend an educational program for college teachers. She will stay in the teachers' hostel for three months.

"This program will be very helpful for us," she remarked.

"How can you say that?" I asked.

"I have read some facts about this program. So I can say that."

On the way to the hostel, we talked about our future.

"I think at the end of this year, we will be able to hold a wedding," she confirmed.

The end of her educational program is the end of this year. Thus, we surely can plan our wedding at the end of the program.

"I want a quiet, small wedding," she said.

"Me, too," I said. I was not telling a lie. I was not saying something false. I was telling the truth. I, like her, really want a quiet wedding.

"I want to invite only a few close friends. It is very tiresome to say thank you, thank you, thank you to so many attendees at weddings," she says, with pretended manner and with pretended sing-song tone of voice. Then she laughs lightly.

We have the same idea for our wedding, because we share the same views on everything. And sometimes I wonder why we have the same views on everything. There must be a certain hidden reason behind this.

When we met for the first time in a café in the town where her college is situated, we talked about some mysterious novels. Maybe it was three or four years ago. I can't remember the year exactly, but I can tell you exactly that it was the most beautiful, bright day I have ever seen or experienced in my life. She was in a pink blouse. I thanked her in my mind for not wearing the red blouse, because red is the color I hate most. I have no reason for hating red. The only reason is that I hate red, because I hate red and because I hate red I hate red.

"Life itself is mysterious," she gave an introductory remark.

"Maybe," I replied, with a nod.

"Not maybe. Exactly, it is," she confirmed her statement. Then she repeated the same words: "Life itself is mysterious." Something in her bright eyes uncovered her strong faith in her words.

I shrugged my shoulders. I had nothing to argue with her. It made no sense to argue with her. I knew well the reason why she has such faith. She told me what happened to her in her previous life. I never heard such stories of reincarnation, but I never heard such a story from the person who can remember his or her previous life. In this very life, she was born as the fifth daughter of a family, in a small town. However, in her previous life she was born as the only daughter of a wealthy family in colonial days in Rangoon, and died as a mother of three daughters and as a granddaughter of six grandchildren in the dictatorship era. She, as a university lecturer, taught English at Rangoon University in the parliamentary era. She, as a wife and mother, led a peaceful and comfortable life before the military coup. But after the military coup, she was no longer a university teacher, and her peaceful and comfortable life ended. Everything changed. Several kinds of hardships entered her life. Her husband was arrested, and never appeared again. She does not remember how old she was when she died. She can't identify the date of her death in previous life. However, it is clear that she died sometime during or a few years before the 1988 revolution, because when the 1988 revolution broke out, she was five. She was born in 1983, and it is a puzzle for her concerning with the life between her death as a grandmother of six grandchildren and her rebirth as the sixth daughter. There might be another life or no other life before she was born in 1983. She cannot remember the gap between her death and this very life. Was she straying here and there as a soul for a few or some or many years?

"I don't remember my daughters' names, but I remember where they live. My parents went there, yet they did not contact my daughters. In reality, everything I am telling you now is what I learnt from my parents. I am not even sure whether all this is true or not.

"My parents went to Rangoon, and investigated everything I told them. At the time, I was young. Maybe I was five or six.

"When I started to talk, I told my mother that in my previous life I was a university lecturer. My mother was so interested in what I said that she asked my name in my previous life. So I told her a name. When she heard the name, she burst out; it is her name. Don't you think it is wonderful? My name in my previous life is identical to my mother's name in this present life of mine. I didn't know my mother's full name."

When she was telling about her past life, I was asking myself many questions about life after death, about reincarnation, about the theory of the cycle of death and rebirth. I don't want to say no to the theory of the cycle of death and rebirth, but I am not ready to say yes to the fact that a person can remember his or her previous life.

Her parents documented everything she told them about her previous life. Everything she told me about her previous life is from the book her parents documented as she had said. If her parents did not exaggerate, everything she told me is correct.

Majority of the people who can remember their previous lives can no longer remember anything about their previous lives after they are ten or so. So it is unusual that she can remember even when she was over ten.

When she told me about her previous life, I did not sense that she was telling me a lie; I did sense she was telling me the truth.

"They seemingly are like motion pictures in my mind. When I read the notebook about my past life, I was amazed. I don't want to believe that it is true. Yet I feel that it is true. It does not matter whether we believe or not," she said.

I said nothing. My mind went back to the time when I told her that I love her. Our beginning was very simple. Like in every love story I have ever read, we two were introduced by my friend at his wedding. We did not know each other before we were introduced by my friend. She did not know that I existed in this country, in this continent, on this earth, in this world. Similarly, I did not know that she existed in this country, in this continent, on this earth, in this world.

What made us meet at my friend's wedding? Was it a well-planned program? Who planned it? I am not sure whose plan this was. However, I am sure this is not my plan. If this is the very beginning of a well-designed plan for two of us, there must be other episode. I don't know the other parts of the plan.

Before being introduced to her, I had no idea that I would be introduced to her. After we had been introduced, I had no idea that we would fall in love each other and became lovers one day. I could not imagine why I paid a visit to my native town and happened to attend his wedding. He did not inform me about his wedding. He did not invite me to attend his wedding. On a whim, I paid a visit to my native town. He did not know beforehand that I would pay a visit. He held his wedding as he had already planned. The result was that we two—my lover and I—met at his wedding. Do we call it coincidence? Do we call it miracle? You can call it as you like. But I think that this is just a simple event. No matter what we call, no matter what I think, it is certain that it really happened.

My friend introduced me to her.

And I came to know who and what she is. She is Miss Moon. (As I have said above, this is the name I gave her. Not her real name.) She is a college teacher. My friend told me that it was her first visit to my native town. She came to attend her friend's wedding: the bride invited her.

She smiled at me. I noticed that her smile made me feel something which I cannot express what it was or what it was like. Everything stopped: time stopped; space stopped; actions stopped; my thoughts stopped. Everything was silent.

"She is an avid reader, like you," my friend said, gesturing towards Miss Moon.

We talked about the books we have read. She has a very good memory and an analytical mind. Right from our first meeting, we became close friends. Strangely, we have the same likes and dislikes, the same view on history, the same view on politics. The only difference between us is sex: she is a woman; I am a man.

"Let me inform you," my friend said, looking at Miss Moon, and then gesturing towards me, he said; "He is very pigheaded."

"Wow, really?" she exclaimed, and then chuckled. "But I don't think he is more pigheaded than I am."

All roared.

Indeed, she is not pigheaded. She is obstinate. She got top marks for every subject when she passed the tenth standard examination. She could be a doctor or an engineer or something like that. But she chose the life of a teacher. Her parents gave no remark about her choice.

Fortunately, we became friends, and two years later I proposed to her. She said yes. We will marry at the end of this year. We decided that we will start a family soon after our marriage. We talked about our wedding on the phone a week before she came to Rangoon.

Wow! Now I remember that I have a cell phone in my trouser pocket. First, I felt my trouser pockets. My right hand felt something in my right trouser pocket. It is my cell phone. I take it out and switch it on. I try to find the phone number of Miss Moon in 'Logs.' Unfortunately, all calls have been deleted. And I try to find the number in 'Contacts'. Fortunately, I find it. Thank. I call her.

"Hello, I am Miss Moon. Who is speaking?" the voice on the other end asks.

My happiness knows no bound. And I answer, "It's me, darling."

"Sorry, who are you?"

I am irritated. Why does she not recognize my voice?

"It's me," raising my voice, I tell her my name.

No sound from her. Certainly she is thinking about my name. A few moments later, I hear her speak.

"Sorry, I don't know this name. Maybe you called the wrong number."

FUCK!

"Where are you now?" I ask. I notice that my tone of voice changes. It is so loud. I sense my nervousness. I should not yell out.

"I am in the City Park," she replies in a normal tone of voice.

I remember that the two of us had made an appointment to meet in the City Park.

"Is there someone with you?"

"Not someone. It is my lover. He is with me."

"Who is he?" I ask.

She tells me a name. It is my name, which makes me worry about her safety.

"Beware, you're in danger now," I warn her.

"What?"

"You're in danger."

"I'm in danger?"

"Yeah, you're in danger."

"OK, I will tell my lover about it."

"No, no. Don't tell him anything. He is not your lover."

"Sorry, I don't understand what you are telling me," she says. Then she hangs up on me.

Why did she hang up on me? I sense grave danger.

I call her. *The number you've dialed is switched off.* A female voice. I try to call her again. *The number you've dialed is switched off.* A female voice again. I try to call her again. *The number you've dialed is switched off.* A female voice again. Did she switch off her phone? It does not make sense for her to switch off her phone. Is it because she wants to switch off or is it because the man by her threatens her to do so? Is she in dilemma over whether to call me as she wants or to switch off as she is being threatened? I am perplexed. I check my phone. No sign of connection. I check the whole room. I see a man speaking on the phone in the right corner of the room. I can't hear what he is saying. But I can judge that this room has a phone connection. If so, why does my phone have no connection? All these confirm my suspicion more. I study the young woman sitting in front of me. No surprise on her face. Surely, she must sense my nervousness. But she shows no sign of sensing my nervousness. Her excellent skill in acting warns me that there is danger. This thought is threatening me all the time. The young woman sitting across me is a danger. The camera operators are a danger. Other workers are a danger. This bleak room is a danger. Everything I experience is a danger.

I need someone's help to escape from this danger. Do I have close friends to ask help from them? I must phone them. OK, 'Contacts' in my phone must have their names. I switch on my phone. No name and number in 'Contacts'. An ominous loss? Recently, I have checked 'Contacts'. There were many names and phone number in 'Contacts'. Now all have been cleared. Who did it? What did it?

"So you mean that you like mystery?"

The question wakes me up. From what she asked, I must have told her something which suggests that I like mystery. I have no reason to deny this. I really like mystery. Should I tell her that not only I, but also my lover loves mystery?

My head rises up and I suddenly look at the young self-possessed woman in the red uniform—the third interviewer. I see her waiting for my answer calmly. She is always surprisingly calm. I envy her calmness, because I am always excited and shocked without any reason. I am sure that she also digs mystery. If I am not wrong, we both talked about mystery two or three days ago. In my mind's eyes, I see the two of us having a hearty conversation about mystery in Café Point, where we frequent. Sometimes she comes with her friend, who told me about her boyfriend. Her boyfriend died of throat cancer five years before our friendship began. I never asked her about her boyfriend. Now the expression on her face shows that she does not know me as her acquaintance, but she knows me as an actor.

"Our knowledge is so limited that we can't understand the things beyond our knowledge." These are the words she told me yesterday. She even looked like a philosopher. She raised her eyebrows and continued, "And we call such things mystery. If the things we call mystery can be solved very easily, they no longer are a mystery."

I was silent. I had nothing to disagree with her.

In truth, I dig mystery. I must admit. But words do not come out of my mouth. Is it because I don't want to admit? I don't think so. To like mystery is not a sin.

When I had a conversation with her in the café, she was not an interviewer. She was my acquaintance. She was a writer. Now she is not my acquaintance. Now she is not a writer. Now she is an interviewer, asking me questions about mystery, about the films, about my ideas, about my other plans.

As far as I can judge, she does not show any sign that she knows me. Why? Does she have amnesia? I don't believe that she does not know me. I think that she is bluffing. Or she really does not know me, or I mistake her for my friend. I am sure that our friendship started two or three years ago. Why does she ignore our friendship? Is it because our friendship is a danger to her?

When I talked with my lover on the phone, I felt excited, annoyed and irritated. I am sure that I can't hide my real emotion. So my emotion will surely appear on my face as expression. And I dare to say that she surely notices it. Nevertheless, the expression on her face is calm. She acts as if she sees no emotion on my face.

What's more, my lover is with someone who will hurt her. She does not recognize my voice. Or she wants to cover reality for her safety or for my safety. Or she does not know me at all. Maybe she thinks that I am with her. I should explain to her everything. But my phone has no connection. I don't know what to do. Do I have nothing to do but to wait for what will happen to us? I can't help her. She can't help me. I can't help myself. One cannot help the other. My lover is in danger, so am I.

I want to ask my acquaintance why she acts as my interviewer. It seems that someone has forced her to do so. Maybe she is under the control of the person. She is not my friend, who is courageous: she is someone else, who is being afraid of something. Anyway, she can conceal her emotion well. I try to summon courage to ask her to tell the truth. To my surprise, I fail.

I start to feel self-doubt. I am not a coward. I can't believe the fact that I fail to ask her to tell the truth. That is not normal. Am I also under pressure? What do they want me to do? What is their real plot? Will my memory be destroyed completely? Will my identity be changed?

"I am your fan. I have watched all the films you starred in. The film I like best is *The Fake* in which you starred as a philosopher. Can you tell me about it?"

The Fake! Is it a code?

Chapter IV
When I Am Silent

"What is the last thing you can remember?"

The question makes a loud noise while there is heavy silence in the room. The question seems to come somewhere far. The question seems to come somewhere nearby. The question seems to come somewhere from inside. The question seems to come somewhere from outside. What does the question mean? What is the meaning of the phrase "the last thing"? This is like the question for an amnesiac. And the questioner seems to treat me as an amnesic. I don't doubt my brain. No fault in my brain. Therefore, no need to doubt the fact that I have no amnesia. I do not feel as if I have awoken from a long sleep. I don't feel that I am still dreaming, not awake. My mind is clear. I remember everything clearly. I can narrate everything in detail, but not in a chronological order, because I remember things, not the chronological order. Perhaps it is because something has sorted the things in my mind by size or by importance, not by date or not by chronology.

That is why it is impossible for me to talk about the last thing I can remember.

In reality, I suspect if I really heard this question, and I ask myself if this can be something in my imagination. I myself don't accept this doubt.

I say to myself that I presume that I heard. I reckon that my ears tell me truth. At the same time, I sense that they make me a fool, giving false information. In what do I believe? In what do I reckon or in what do I sense? Sometime what we perceive fools us. So it might be that I am fooled by my perception of hearing.

My mind confirms that I heard a question and it is me who asked. Is my mind telling the truth or telling a lie? No doubt. I am sure that this is what I really heard. At the same time, I can't believe in what my mind tells me. OK. Who is the questioner? Me? One of the young women? Someone else? No one? Unfortunately, I am not sure whether I am not sure. In fact this is not the first time I feel uncertain about what I have encountered recently. I am used to feeling uncertain. To feel uncertain is part of my life. Or I am uncertainty.

I am the type of person who always feels uncertain about what he experiences. I have no idea why I am such a person. Perhaps I was born as such a person or perhaps I was shaped to be such a person by my environment, by my education or by the age I have to pass through. I am not trying to flee from reality and responsibility. I am not brave, yet I am not a coward, who fears to face reality and responsibility. I never ran away from reality and responsibility.

I warn myself that there might be a certain reason hidden from me. My knowledge is limited. Everyone's knowledge is limited. Your knowledge is limited. You are not allowed to know anything beyond the horizon of your knowledge. And so, some important reasons are hidden from us, from our knowledge. What we know are what we are allowed to know. However, we are proud of ourselves for knowing this, for knowing that. We don't let the others know that there are things we don't know, that there are things beyond our horizon of knowledge. It is not unusual.

Now I feel something is hidden. This hidden thing is what exists beyond our knowledge. This hidden thing is what we are not allowed to know.

I study the young woman in the pink uniform. She remains silent. It seems that she has remained silent for so long for several reasons. I see no expression on her face, so it is hard for me to guess what she is wondering or what she is feeling. Why does she remain silent? Perhaps it is because she is in deep thought. Perhaps it is because she has nothing to say. Perhaps it is because she is in a bad mood. Perhaps it is because she wants to be quiet.

I can't recall the first sentence of this conversation. There are many things I remember, but the first sentence is the exception. Did we start our conversation with the expression like, *I am glad to have a conversation with you?* I am sure I am not glad. This conversation is a hell to me.

I don't want to store her questions in my memory. I don't want to keep my answers in my memory. I want to erase everything. I want to drive everything out of my memory. However, I fail to erase some questions and answers. The first sentence may be one of some questions and answers I could erase.

"So it is not surprising that you are more popular than the other actors."

This sentence occurs to me. It is what she concluded one or two hours ago. I cannot recollect what I told her or what she asked me. This conclusion must relate to her question and to my answer. From my answer, she drew this conclusion. Probably she asked me a short question and I gave a long answer, which might be an evidence for her to draw such an *easy* conclusion. I use the adjective 'easy' here, because I feel that she drew this conclusion without deep consideration or contemplation. To draw a conclusion is not an easy task. I abhor the act of drawing a conclusion easily, without concrete evidences, without serious pondering. I have never met many people who draw conclusion without meditating on the issue seriously.

More popular than other actors. This implies that I am an actor and I am the most popular among fellow actors. To me it is like humor which can't make anyone laugh. I am not an actor. It is impossible for me to be more popular than other actors, far from it! It is impossible for me to be popular even as an actor. I am certain that I never dreamt of being an actor, because I saw that I had no talent to be an actor, and I was not interested in acting.

My mind goes back to the past hour or two ago.

She (the second interviewer) told me that *Escape,* in which I starred as a young man who lives life in a carefree way of style and who revolts the established norms of the society, can attract the public so much. Once I heard the word 'escape', I felt something. Surprise? Joy? Excitement? Bewilderment? I could not imagine what it was. I told myself that I had nothing to do with *Escape*, but I felt that I had something to do with *Escape*. There must be a relationship between *Escape* and me. The problem was that I could not uncover it. At any rate, I would not give up trying to find it.

Surely I know the meaning of the word 'escape', but I do not know what *Escape* means to me.

I saw a young man running through the flame: it was me. I saw a young man reading a script: it was me. I saw a young man saying something to a camera operator: it was me. I heard someone yell, "ACTION!" I heard someone yell, "CUT!" Was it in a shooting that I saw and heard these things? I saw a woman of about fifty. She was saying things to others, including camera operators. She held a file of papers in her right hand. I could not hear well what she was saying. I noticed that everyone paid respect to her. She was not a stranger to me, yet I could not figure out who and what she was. It seemed that she had influence on all of us.

I happened to ask myself why I felt like that and why I saw such things one after another. I saw some pictures, too. I heard some voices, too. I could not stop them. Pictures and voices came into my mind's eyes, into my mind's ears. I was so powerless that I could not drive them out or stop them. I could not direct my mind. My mind did not obey my order. I ordered my mind not to see these things and not to hear these things, but it disobeyed.

I saw a young, beautiful woman (I called her Miss Beauty, later I will tell you why I called her so.) of my own age. She was sitting by me on a bench. The two of us were having a conversation. We were like lovers. We were talking about something serious. The tone of our voices was serious. Our manners were serious. Expressions on our faces were serious. I saw her leading the conversation. I heard the voice, "CUT!" And she stopped talking. The camera operators changed the angles. Then I heard the voice, "ACTION!" And then we restarted our conversation.

I try to remember the things we talked in our conversation and the actions we performed. Fortunately, I can recall some words we spoke and some actions we performed, even things in my mind.

"We must risk," I warned Miss Beauty.

"Of course, we must," she agreed. "We have no option. But I believe that we will be able to overcome it."

"How?"

"I have no idea, but I am sure we can."

I saw her laughing lightly. It was the sign of showing indifference to danger. I tried to see something in her tone of voice and words. But I saw nothing.

I heard someone say, "CUT!" again. And we stopped talking. She smiled at me and said so quietly that no one could hear what she said.

"You did well."

I tried to realize what her smile and what her words meant. A smile is a smile is a smile. I stopped searching for the meaning of her smile. She smiled, because she wanted to smile. She said, "You did well," because she wanted to say, "You did well." That's all.

I came to notice that the bench on which we were sitting was located in a ranch where I had never been before. But I sensed that I had seen it in a film or in a dream. I heard no sounds of vehicles. So I guessed that this place must be far from a city or far from even a highway road. I felt annoyed, but her expression showed that she felt excited.

"You did well," Miss Beauty said solemnly.

It seemed that the conversation restarted. The expression on her face changed. She was acting as though she would have to make a very important decision. I tried to repress the impulse to laugh out loud.

I had no idea what "You did well" really meant. She said, "You did well." Two times: first, quietly and second, solemnly. Which carried what meaning?

What did I do? What did I do? What did I do?

I managed to calm myself down. But I could not help asking.

Were these the scenes from *Escape*?

The scene changed. The young, beautiful woman and I were walking side-by-side. I looked here and there. I saw no camera operator and no other people who worked together with them. I could not understand what was happening to me. I could not believe what was happening to me. Why were the two of us alone?

She looked sidelong at me and said, "We're free now."

"We're free now," I echoed.

What did it mean? I struggled to figure out the real meaning of the sentence. Especially the word 'free' inserted some difficult questions into my mind. Would she tell me what it was if I asked her? I did not want to ask. I wanted to find out the answer myself. To have answer, I must go back to the deep past. I could not go back to the deep past. All I could do was, but decode the meaning of pictures I had seen and the meanings of sounds and voices I had heard.

We seemed to be controlled by something or someone powerful. We seemed to be forced to do things. We seemed to be victims. We seemed to be hostages. We seemed to be prisoners. Finally I decided to ask her.

"What do you mean by, '*We're free now*'?"

She gave a light laugh and said: "Simple. '*We're free now*' means, '*We're free now*'. That's all." She shrugged her shoulders and lifted her eyebrows. I tried to interpret her manners and tone of voice. They seemed to indicate that we were safe. And the word 'free' could be interpreted as 'safe' here, in this context. It might have the other meaning according to the other context. Meaning of this word could change, depending on the context.

I could not imagine why she said so? Was it because we had been kidnapped somewhere by criminals for some reasons? Was it because we had been arrested for committing a crime. If we were arrested for a criminal case, surely it was because we were framed. And another question was: free from what? I found myself being busy with questions without answer.

"Sometimes I want to walk like this, without fear, without worry, without care, without burden. I like walking."

"So do I. Walking is a good exercise."

"I like walking not because walking is a good exercise, but because while walking I can envision a world I want to live in."

"Unless you don't walk for exercise, then for what do you walk?"

"For pleasure."

"For pleasure?"

"Yes, for pleasure," she replied. Then she explained, "We need time for pleasure just as we need time for meal."

I nodded and said yes. I thought I agreed with her. But I never imagined anything while walking. My '*So do I*' was just a lie: I was not sure if I liked walking as she did. I must confess that I never enjoyed walking. I did not even know that from walking we can get pleasure.

She was walking in a carefree manner. I envied her carefree manner. I had something to worry, I had something to fear. My mind was not free like hers. While walking, I was someone else. I was somewhere else, with a heavy burden on my mind, with a heavy burden in my heart.

"In fact, life is full of miseries. Life is suffering," she said in a tone of drawing a conclusion. In her tone of voice, I detected her way of seeing things. She views things from a pessimistic aspect. I did not feel that my life, as she concluded, was full of miseries. I had times to enjoy life, though I had things to worry about.

"Key point is to ask ourselves," she said in a tone of a preacher or of a psychotherapist. I had no desire to clash with her on this issue though I had different views. I told myself in my mind that perhaps she read Greek tragedy a lot and believed in Greek tragedy a lot. I had no idea why she kept such a pessimistic view of life. I also read Greek tragedy a lot, but I did not see life as suffering, as she did. It was strange that she had a pessimistic view, but her way of living life was very light. Or my conclusion that she had a pessimistic view might be wrong. Or she had two opposite views of life. Or she had split-personalities.

"What should we ask ourselves?"

"About what we can do and about what we cannot do," she paused and was wondering about something she was going to say. She was choosing the right words very carefully. Now she was like a good writer. No doubt, she was a good speaker. A few moments later, she continued: "There are things we can't change. There are things we can change. Miseries we encountered are the things we can't change. They have already happened to us. We can change feelings and emotions caused by miseries. Miseries which happened to us are causes, and the feelings and emotions caused by them are the consequences. We can't change causes, but we can change consequences."

"You might be right," I said, but I had a different view.

"I suppose you should try it."

I shrugged my shoulders. "Do you believe that I am strong enough to change such results?"

"Surely, I do."

At the crossroads, she turned left into another road and walked north. I never heard the name of this road. I never saw this scene. I did not tell her about it. But I happened to ask.

"Where are we going?"

"Somewhere," she answered, "we are going for a walk just for pleasure, not for a business matter. So to where, is not important."

I could say nothing but nodded.

I did not let her know that I was skeptical about what she was saying.

Now we were at the outskirts of the town. In front of my eyes, there was an endless moor. I did not guess where I was, because I realized that I could not guess rightly where I was. As far as I could, I found myself somewhere I had never been before. I felt scared. Judging from the expression on her face, this might be a place she frequented.

"I love looking at the space like this."

I did not say '*So do I*', because I was not sure.

She, like a teenage girl, was spinning, yelling out meaningless words such as, 'Woo... Woo... Woo... Aah... Aah... Aah...' uttering some phrases: "OK, let it be. Beware of shadow. I make myself ready. It is time..."

Her words were puzzles for me. I tried to decode them first, but I came to see that I could do nothing, and gave up decoding.

There was no one here but the two of us. There was nothing here but sky and horizon. The spectacle I was witnessing was really surreal. I felt as if we were in a surrealist painting. My fear was lost. I found myself nowhere. Fortunately, our cell phones were silent. No one called us. Maybe it was because of a lack of connection. I heard the breeze blowing tenderly.

There was nothing which would disturb our great moment of solitude.

My mind comes back to the present. Now all those voices and pictures disappear. I try to see them again. But I fail. I feel that I am intimate with the young actress I saw in my mind. My memory brings me a name—Miss Beauty. If I am right, she must be a famous actress. Why did I find myself with a famous actress in a shooting and somewhere like that? I have no answer. I can visualize her in my mind. She has an oval-shaped face and dark shoulder-length hair. She has thick eyebrows and a small dimple on the right cheek. She has sparkling eyes and thin red lips. She is beautiful, so I called her Miss Beauty.

The pictures, sounds and voices came into my mind without my knowledge, without my permission. They went out of my mind without my knowledge, without my permission. It was as if my mind was not my mind. I was eager to listen to what Miss Beauty would say next. But the scene I saw disappeared. The sounds and voices I heard also disappeared. I had no chance to hear what she would say next. And the thought, from what she told me, maybe I would get a clue to solve this morass, too, ended in vain.

I want to go back to the time when we met and conversed. I want to go back to the place where we met and conversed. She must have many things to tell me. I want to be back on the moor with her again. I try to imagine the moor. Damn it. I can't send my mind to the moor. I can't visualize the moor.

Now I have no clue. In my mind I try to locate the place where we both were then, I fail. I don't know where I am now. All I know is that it is a large room. I don't know what happened to me then. I can't imagine what is happening to me now. Without any clue, I will not be able to figure out what will happen to me next. Even the thing I am going to encounter one or two minutes later is hidden from me, from my knowledge. It is unfair that I am not allowed to know beforehand, what is going to happen to me so soon, in a few seconds. If it is a danger that I am going to encounter, I have no time or no way to try to get out of that danger. When I become aware that it is danger, I will find myself in danger. It is too late for me to avoid the danger.

If I have chance, I will try to uncover the one steering this morass. He put these fucking things into my mind as he wished. Then he took these fucking things out of my mind as he desired. He is abusing my mind as he likes. I must stop him. The problem is that I have no idea how to stop him. At any rate, I must not give up. I must stand up to whatever happened, happens and will happen to me. I must be strong enough to face anything without fear.

"I like *Escape* so much," the first interviewer sitting in front of me restarts the conversation. She stopped the conversation for some minutes for some reasons. I am not sure how many questions she has already asked me, and how many answers I have already given to her. The other young women, too, have conversed with me. They asked me questions and I answered. I did not get annoyed with them for torturing me by asking questions. I understand them. I sense that they, too, are forced to ask questions, to treat me like this. I detect fear in their eyes though they try to hide it. Their faces show no sign of fear or any emotion. But they cannot hide the emotions in their eyes. They are good at posing as interviewers. They are good at pretending to be unfamiliar with me. But they are not good at hiding their fear. Or maybe, I am good at detecting fear in their eyes. What I must do now is to do as they want me to do. I must forget everything. I am the one who they want me to be. It is not an easy task for me.

"Might *Escape* be a milestone in your career as an actor?"

I hear the first interviewer ask me a question, which astonishes and bewilders me so much that I cannot imagine what I should answer. She should pose other questions. She should not ask the questions which trap me.

"No, no. Not a milestone. My view is something else."

I curse myself for my abrupt, reckless answer. I don't have enough knowledge about *Escape*. All I learnt about *Escape* (I am not sure whether I learnt about *Escape* from her or from my own experience) is that it is a film in which I starred as a young man who lives life in a carefree way of style and who revolts against the established norms of the society. I, therefore, should be silent. Or I must ask her first to tell me about *Escape* in detail as far as she can.

"Do you have a certain reason to say so?" she asks, casting a glance at me.

"Of course, I do."

She gestures for me to tell her about the reason.

"I don't believe in milestones," I say. I am aware that my tone is a bit brusque. I have already said, though I know I should not say so. I can do nothing. I can't take back what I have already said.

She smiles. It is a mysterious smile the meaning of which I can't decode. Perhaps it is a mocking smile. Perhaps it is a pleased smile. Perhaps it is a displeased smile. Perhaps it is a surprised smile.

"OK, if so, in what do you believe?"

Her question demands time to meditate deeply. In reality, I have never even asked myself such a question. So I do not have an exact answer for that question. I have no idea in what I do believe. The real answer in my mind is that I don't believe in anything. But I put a brake on my thought in time and thank myself a lot.

"Sorry, I am not sure whether I have something in which I believe."

I sense that she is not satisfied with my answer.

"You do not mean that you do not believe in anything. Don't you?"

"No. I mean I am not sure whether I have something in which I believe."

"Do you live with doubts and uncertainties?"

"I didn't say it like that. I don't see any word which may lead to misconception like this."

"OK, let's return to our main subject," she advises. Then she asks me some questions about my views on *Escape.*

"In *Escape*, you starred as a young man who challenges established norms of the society. You were a rebel in *Escape*," she puts stress on the word 'rebel'.

"Maybe I am a rebel in *Escape* according to what you say."

"Not according to what I say, but according to the character you played in *Escape*."

"OK, I am a rebel according to the character I played in *Escape*."

"And in your real life?"

"Sorry, I never asked myself such a question."

"Do you mean that you are not sure if you're a rebel or not?"

"Exactly."

"So, what type of a person are you?"

I shrug my shoulders and say: "I am afraid, I have no idea. Maybe I am the one who does not know himself."

She laughs heartily. So do I. This short moment is free from all kinds of worries. Her hearty laugh melts my worries. I feel lightness at the very moment. But I am not sure how long it will last. This moment has a meaning to me. Thus, I want to prolong this precious moment.

According to the words of the young woman, I am a brave, young man who loves freedom in *Escape*. However, I am not such a brave, young man in real life. In real life, I always run away from freedom. According to the words of the young woman, I am a courageous young man in *Escape*. However I am a coward in real life. In real life, I always shun the tasks which demand courage.

The names of the famous actors and actresses show up in my mind. I have stored them in my memory for a long time. For what purpose did I keep their names in my memory? For future use? To my astonishment, the name of the actress who was with me does not show up in my mind. Why? I don't want to reflect on *why* right now.

Once I utter the name of an actress, the films in which she starred occur to me. I can tell you the synopsis of those films. I can tell you about those films in detail. This proves that I have interest in watching films and in analyzing films. Surprisingly, I have no interest in acting.

I never wanted to be popular as an actor. So it is no doubt that I would not try to be an actor. I love a simple, quiet way of life, an ordinary life, a carefree life. To me, to be popular is to be in prison or to lose freedom. It is also a threat. I have read the books about popular people. The more they became popular, the more they lost their freedom. Great gain and great loss. I don't want to lose my freedom. I love freedom. I love a carefree way of life.

Did I tell someone that I love a carefree way of life? Whom? When? Where? Why? I get no answer. My good memory is no longer good and does not work well now.

I feel drowsy. I guess it is about five or six hours that we have been sitting here in this large room. I have answered many questions from four young women, in four different uniforms. They forgot their identities. I wonder whether they love their new identities. I don't see any sign of feeling and emotion on their faces. They are good at hiding feeling and emotion. They seem to be trained well to do so. The expressions on their faces are like the expressions on the dead. They are straight-faced. Even while I tell jokes, they do not laugh, they do not smile. They speak in a monotone. No intonation at all. When they say something, I feel icy.

Now they say nothing. She says nothing. I feel that they all are watching me silently. So there is silence, heavy silence, icy silence, dreadful silence, boring silence. I like silence, but not a silence like this. I don't like this silence. To me this silence symbolizes danger or threat. I want to break this silence as quickly as I can. To break silence I must have a phrase like 'by the way' at least. However, I have no phrase, no word. I am not good enough to break silence and restart the conversation. I am not a good speaker who can lead or restart the conversation.

From my mother I learnt that I started to speak only when I was six. Too bad. She did not know why I was late to speak. Everyone thought that I would never speak, but my mother could not accept the thought that I was speech impaired. When I started to speak at age six, she rejoiced so much. She told everyone that her son could speak well. Nobody could believe in what she said, because everyone in my small quarter assumed that I was speech impaired. And they thought that my mother had gone mad. And when they came to see the truth, they were surprised. However, they did not show any sign of surprise or joy. They remained as if they felt nothing strange. Later, I came to have a suspicion that they wanted me to be dumb and that they enjoyed my dumbness. And I had to drive my suspicion out of my mind. It was a painstaking task. My suspicion was rooted in my mind. Every word they said, every look they gave, was a root cause to arise my suspicion. Having suspicion was a heavy burden to me. I knew I should drop it, but I could not.

I tell the young woman in the grey uniform about my childhood briefly.

"Incredibly, I knew many big words at age six when I started to speak."

The young woman shows no sign of surprise. The other young women, too, remain silent, with no sign of surprise on their faces. It is as if they have already heard about it. It is as if they hear $1+2 = 3$ or it is as if they hear nothing. I am astonished, because they are not astonished. Maybe, it is not because they didn't hear what I said that they show no sign of surprise. If so, why? I can't imagine why. Anyway to tell them about my talent is my business. To believe or not in what I say, is their business. We do our own businesses. A murder kills: to kill is his business. A physician saves: to save is his business. A dictator oppresses people: to oppress people is his business. A leader leads people: to lead people is his business. A preacher preaches. To preach is his business. At this point, my business is to tell them about my language talent. They may assume that I am making a story. No matter. I am on my side to state that I am telling the truth.

"The words which I was very familiar with at age six were the ones a six-year-old boy could not be familiar with," I pause and study the young women. They remain silent, no expression on their faces. It is hard for them to believe the fact that I am telling the truth. However, they, as I have said above, seem to misunderstand that I am inventing a story to persuade them to admire me for my great talent. I don't want to impress. I just want them to see the truth about me and want them to accept it as the truth. I have language talent. That is truth. And I want them to see it, to accept it. That's all.

And I continue, "While the other boys of my age did not know the meaning of the word 'poverty', I knew its meaning. I learnt the meaning of *poverty* not from books, but from my experience, not only as a word but as reality. I was born where poverty dominated. I grew up where poverty overwhelmed. I saw poverty in my own eyes, not in the dictionaries but in my small town. People, including my parents, lived in poverty. To me the word 'poverty' is more than *a situation in which someone does not have enough money to pay for their basic needs* as defined in the dictionary. I was born together with poverty. I grew up together with poverty. Poverty was my playmate. Poverty was my partner. Poverty was my textbook. Poverty came with its partners. Because of poverty, all of this happened in my small quarter. Parents had no interest in education. For them, education was for the rich, not for the poor like them. They could not afford to school their children. The children had to leave school very early at the primary level and became child workers.

"When the 1988 revolution broke out, they had no radio, they had no newspaper. Majority of people in our small quarter were uneducated and idiotic. They had no knowledge about politics. They had no knowledge about education. They never blamed our BSPP government for the poverty and illiteracy. They did not even know that the government was responsible for the people's poverty and illiteracy. I must admit that they were more idiotic than I can say. They took it that they were poor and uneducated, because of the bad deeds they had performed in their previous lives. So they blamed their past bad deeds for their poverty and illiteracy. They saw themselves as the culprits for their poverty and illiteracy."

The interviewers respond nothing to what I have said. Maybe they have no interest in what I have said. Maybe it is hard for them to accept what I said as truth. Anyway, I believe that my words, though they are boring, put a thought into their minds. Their silence bears witness to their thoughtfulness. In truth, this is my one-sided view. The reality might be something else. Perhaps it is because they are so bored that they remain silent, without giving any comment. I hope a comment or exclamation from them.

"Incredible!"

"Really?"

"What the hell on earth!"

"This is a threat to the country."

"Nonsense!"

I must admit that what I have said deviated from the main subject of our conversation. I did not mean it to. According to my words, I was a very intelligent boy. Yes, that I was a very intelligent boy, is the fact. But in their view, it is not fact, but a fiction I create, because I want to impress.

I cannot guarantee that what I experienced in my life is a fascinating story. But I can guarantee that what I encountered in my life may differ from what my respected interviewers encountered. I, therefore, want to share my stories. And I wait for the time when they will give me the green light.

I get a fleeting glimpse of the serene expression on her face. It seems to mean that she is meditating on something serious. I cannot say exactly about what she is pondering. Maybe she is wondering about the present situation, the mess for me and the blessing for her. Maybe she is wondering about me. Maybe she is wondering about herself. Maybe she is wondering about something else. Maybe she is thinking about not thinking, too.

I attempt to announce my real identity, but I fail. This is not the first attempt. This is not the first failure. Whenever I tried, I felt that I was threatened to keep silent about the truth. Fear overwhelmed me. Now it is time for me to give up my failed attempt and to accept their invented reality.

You may regard me as the guy who does not dare to admit his weakness. I am not brave, yet I am not a coward. I have enough courage to prove that I am mistaken for an actor. To do this, I need files about my real identity. My identity card is the best proof. I can't imagine why I forgot the fact that I have an identity card. I will show them my identity card, which will convince them of who and what I really am. I search for my identity card in my trouser pockets, then in my purse and then in my backpack. I find it nowhere. I have no identity card with me. Maybe I left it in the drawer of my writing table. I always take it with me wherever I go. And probably my identity card was stolen, which means that my identity was stolen.

Now I need the help of a close confidante, who will bear witness to my real identity. I remember a name. It might be a name of my close confidante. I utter the name in low tone. Immediately, a face appears in my mind's eyes. She is the young woman who is sitting in front of me. She is the first interviewer. I am surprised. This implies that my close confidante is now trying to hide my real identity and treating me as someone else. Or this implies that my close confidante is the one who forgets even her own identity. I don't feel that she is my close confidante. The information given by my memory is questionable. Is my memory giving me false information? What's more, even my memory is questionable. This is the very first time that I start to doubt my memory. Regrettably, the one my memory recommends as my close confidante, is the one I can't trust.

Who are the other confidantes? No name nor face occurs to me. It is impossible that I have no other confidantes. The information about my confidantes kept in my memory seemed to be hacked to pieces recently.

What can I do for me now? Must I say a prayer for help? For what must I say a prayer? Who will answer my prayer? What will answer my prayer? I don't want to accept the fact that I am powerless. I have power. I will surely overcome this mess. I must take time. Time will come to me. I must get out of this mess. I must find out the things which can testify my real identity.

Just by saying, *I am not who you think I am, or I am not the actor as you think*, I will not be out of this mess.

I must be patient. I must show tolerance. Time to find the way will come. As there is time for me to be in this mess, there must be time for me to get out of this mess. This is what I believe.

What I don't believe is this: it is impossible to get out of this mess. Now it is time for me to draw a plan in my mind. To do this I must empty my mind first.

Now I come to see that the first interviewer is not my close confidante I see in my memory. She is someone else. My memory is playing a game. At present, I can't recall her name. All I can recall is this: she is a successful sales manager from a famous company, not an interviewer. A friend of mine who works in the same company introduced me to her, two or three years ago, in a poetry reading at an art gallery. We became friends. We exchange knowledge. We exchange views. We exchange feelings. We exchange stories about our lives. I confided in her, she confided in me. Now she really forgets or pretends to forget the relationship between the two of us. To forget our close relationship totally, her brain must be damaged badly, and she must have amnesia. And now the question is: how her brain was damaged badly? As far as I know, everything is okay in her life. Though she had to lead a hard life before, she leads an easy life now. She does not have much to worry about. She does not have much to stress about. So even if her brain was damaged badly, it is obvious that worry and stress were not the causes of such damage. What if she hid her worry and stress from me? That would be an exception.

Say, that her brain was damaged in a car accident. If I remember correctly, we met two or three days ago and talked about contemporary literature over coffee. If she was hurt in a car accident after that, she must be in the hospital right now, not here, in this room. Accordingly, it must be concluded that her brain was not damaged at all, and she did not have amnesia at all.

If she does not have amnesia, she will not mistake me for someone. In my view, she is not pretending to have amnesia, she is pretending to be someone else and she is making me accept that she is someone else. She must have a certain reason for doing so. I have no intention to ask her what it is. If I am right, she is under pressure from someone who is intimidating her.

It is unusual that she is afraid of someone. I have no doubt that she is brave. Any hardship of life could not stop her. Once, when she was in a good mood, she told my friend, my friend's girlfriend and me about her girlhood. "I had no good friend," she said, touching the rim of the coffee cup with her right index finger. "No one wanted to be my friend. First I felt lonely and depressed, yet later I started to hate others. I did not want to make friends with other girls. In my eyes, they were bitches, they were cunning. I sensed that they were waiting for the chance to humiliate me." Her voice sank when she uttered the word 'humiliate'. I know the dictionary definition of *humiliate*, nevertheless it was impossible for me to understand the real meaning of *humiliate* or to understand how she felt when she was *humiliated*, because it was not me who was *humiliated* and I had never been humiliated.

"I was humiliated several times," she said in a low tone. "Unfortunately, I was poor. Fortunately, I was bright. I did not want to be first in class. Fortunately or unfortunately, I was always first in class. And they envied me and tried to annoy me by various means. They always victimized me."

"Yes, I do understand how you felt," I said. In fact, I did not understand how she felt. I was poor like her. But I was not a bright student. I was not first in my class and I did not want to be first in class. So no one envied me and I envied no one. No one annoyed me and I annoyed no one. Hence to say, *I do understand how you felt* is partly to tell a lie. How can I understand how she felt without experiencing what she experienced?

"My handwriting was beautiful."

Her eyes were bright when she said that. I instinctively sensed her honesty.

"My handwriting was ugly," I said, shrugging my shoulders.

"And I was told to write on the black board."

Great! I was never asked by any teacher to do so. This was what I told myself in my mind. I feared that she would misinterpret my word as a mockery of her skill. I had no will to mock her. I really admire her. I must confess that she impressed me a lot.

"They did not like it. Surely, they wanted me to be stupid, idiotic. Being bright was my fault."

"I remember a title of a novel written by a famous Burmese novelist."

"What is it?"

"If I remember correctly, it is like this: *Some Likes Idiots*. You are not an idiot. So they don't like you. It is so simple."

Her lips curled. "I did my best as I believed. Was that a mistake?"

I notice that her tone of her voice changed. I felt something ironic in her tone of voice. It came from her trauma. No doubt that she was beaten by the various kinds of blows, which shaped her as a brave, young woman.

"But now I try to lead an easy life."

It was two or three days ago that the four of us had this conversation over coffee. A few minutes later, the subject of our conversation changed. We talked about contemporary literature. She is a very critical reader. She remembers everything she has read. She has a very good memory.

As I remember everything, she should to. Her memory is better than mine. At that time she was in a medical company's uniform. Now she is in a TV channel's uniform. I see a logo and the name of the TV channel on her badge. I have never heard of such a TV channel. Is it a false channel? Strangely, I don't see the name on her badge.

I tell myself that I should accept what happens to me. And I say; no.

My mind goes back to the café.

"Some said that I am very pigheaded," she said, with a half-laughing tone of voice. "I have no idea why they made such a conclusion."

"Maybe it is because you don't listen to others' tips?"

"Probably not."

I don't remember why the four of us met that day. Especially since we only met at weekends. Surely, that day was not a weekend, because she was in uniform. Was there something in our conversation that I forgot? It must be a very serious issue we discussed that day. What was it? I remember everything but the serious issue. Is it because a small part of my memory is damaged? And what about her memory?

Anyway, I must thank myself as my entire memory has not been damaged and hacked. Now if she believes or not, I must tell her that the four of us met two or three days ago in a café. She may suspect that I am inventing a story. That's her business. My business is to convince her that all of us are in trouble, with false identities.

At this point, the problem is that I have nothing to prove that I am telling the truth. But if I can call my friend and my friend's girlfriend to come here, they will be able to prove that she is a sale manager, not an interviewer. To do this I must have my friend's phone number, and I must tell him where I am. I have no idea where I am. All I can say is that I am in a large room where I have never been before.

I need my friend's help. Everyone in this room is unreliable. To ask for help from anyone in this room is to beckon danger. No one in this room will be on my side. Now no one shows menace. But if I ask for help, everyone will show menace.

I feel that I am being watched. I am not safe. They can hurt me any time, but I can't hurt them at all. This is unfair. But I have no right to say that this is unfair. My right is nothing here and now. Even the word *right* is nothing more than a word. To speak honestly, I am living in a country where the word *right* does not work. Even the term *human right* remains inactive, invalid here, in this country.

Who is responsible for this mess? The question stirs indignation in my mind. I try my best to suppress my emotion. I must be controlled so that I can handle this desperate situation. I must seek the way. Surely, there is the way. I do not believe that there is no way.

I must call my friend first. I hope he will able to persuade her that we are not those she thinks we are. I put my hands into my trouser pockets. My hands feel nothing in the pockets. I remember that I called someone and had a short phone conversation. Before I could not finish my sentence, the one on the other side hanged up on me. This is what I remember well. I am sure that it was a woman I had talked on phone with, but I am not sure who she was. Now I cannot find my cell phone. I should find my cell phone easily. This shows that that the memory that I had phone conversation with a woman is merely my imagination.

Where is my cell phone? I see a backpack besides me. And I zip it open. I put my right hand into it and search for my cell phone. My hand feels something hard. My cell phone. I take it out. Then I switch it on. I search for my friend's name and number in the contacts. All names and numbers in the contacts are new to me. And I conclude that this is not my cell phone.

However, I can't say that the backpack is not mine. The backpack is mine. I take out all the contents. Surely each is belongs to me: the book, the purse, the hat etc. Maybe someone took my cell phone and put his or hers into my backpack. Why did they do it? Fortunately, I remember my number. And I check the number. The same number I remember. If so, I must accept that this is my cell phone. No, the number is mine and the handset is someone else's. Maybe handsets were exchanged. It is strange that the brand of handset is the same. Even the handset's color is the same. My SIM card was put into another identical handset with the same brand, of the same size, and the same color. If this handset is mine, the names and numbers in it should not be lost. The unknown names and numbers should not be in it. Did someone delete all the old numbers in the contacts and in the call log and put new phone numbers in the contacts and in the call log instead? All phone numbers in the call log are the ones I never called. I don't even know those names and numbers. What will happen to me if I call one of those numbers? Should I try it? No, I should not. The mess will become double. It might be another trap. I put everything, including the cell phone, into my backpack and zip it shut.

I put the cell phone into my backpack. (I know I should check the other things such as Gallery, My Files, Music etc. in this handset, but I fail to check. I don't know why.) Then I study her. It seems that she pays no attention to any performance of mine. She keeps writing on her laptop, ignoring me and my presence. I notice camera operators shooting from different angles. They are performing their duties, like dutiful robots. They all evade my look. It is obvious that they fear that their eyes and my eyes will meet and that I will come to see their mind through their eyes. This is what I believe. The reality might be, that to them I am nothing more than an object to shoot. They shoot me, yet they do not look at me. Their eyes are just for adjusting camera angles, not for looking at me.

Even if I remember my friend's phone number and call him, I cannot tell him where I am, and so he will not be able to locate me. I order my mind to calculate the possibilities.

The first thing I must do is to find out the exact location of this tall building. Is this building located in the town I live, or somewhere else? If this building is a high-rise apartment building, then this building is located somewhere else.

The room is so large. It is about sixty by eighty feet, I guess. This room might be one of the many rooms in a flat and this flat is one of the many flats of a huge high-rise. I have no idea how many feet tall this building is. I have no idea how many feet wide this building is. I have no idea how many flats this building has. From seeing the width and height of the room, I judge that this is a grand high-rise building with many apartments. I might be right. I might be wrong.

I want to warn her that she is not an interviewer. I want to tell her that she is forced to act as an interviewer. Astonishingly, all these things are lost in my thoughts. They don't come out. Surely, it is because I can't take her as my confidante now. Or it is because I fear something. This makes me nervous. I am not prepared to accept this. Even I am being forced to be immobile and to keep quiet.

I want to tell her everything I know about her. She tried very hard to be a sales manager of the company. To others to be a sales manager may be easy, but to her to be a sales manager was not so easy. When she passed the eighth standard examination, she had no chance to attend the ninth standard: her mother could not afford. She had to quit school and worked as a laborer. One year later, her relatives—they also were not well to do—gave financial support to her to go to school. When she passed the ninth standard exam, she got a contract with an education foundation. She sat for an entrance exam to be the student of the foundation. Fortunately, she passed. And so the foundation helped her to attend the tenth standard. She, after passing the tenth standard exam, worked two years as a sales girl at a store. On the weekends, she attended private classes. It was in this way that she became a sales manager.

She can stand any hardship in her life. Any failure could not move her. Her father died in a car accident two weeks before she was born. And she grew up as a fatherless child. She, having no photo of her father, couldn't visualize her father. Her father's image she drew in her mind was like an image made of smoke. She could not finish the image. I would like to tell her that I can understand a fatherless child's life. This does not mean that I was born and grew up as a fatherless child like her.

Can I really understand a fatherless child's life? If I say yes, it would be just a lie. I am not a fatherless child. So it is impossible to understand a fatherless child's life. My understanding might be superficial.

It was when I was twenty-five that my father died. My father was famous for being very pigheaded, and I inherited this fame from my father. Unfortunately, my father did not have a good education. Fortunately, he had a good memory. Whenever he was in a good mood, he told me about his childhood, boyhood and everything he experienced. His parents had seven children, and he was the eldest son.

"Your father was indulged by his aunts so much," my mother told me about my father two months after his death. We were talking about something else. She changed the main subject of our talk suddenly. It was her habit to change the subject of the talk suddenly. So I was not surprised that she started to tell me about my father without any introduction. I told myself that she seemed to have a special reason to do so. Her look was so serene.

My father had three aunts from his mother's side. I never saw them because they passed away some years ago before I was born. They were all spinsters who lived lives happily. When my mother conceived me, she saw my father's youngest aunt in her dream. She was in a white dress. With a very bright smile on her face, she told my mother to let her be my mother's son. My mother was so pleased that she could not say anything but giving a nod. It seemed to mean permission. The next morning, my mother informed everything in her dream to my dad, who did not believe. His reason was so simple.

"My aunt, you know, passed away six years ago. And now she might be a five-year-old girl or boy."

"I don't want to quarrel with you on this issue, but I can say that she told me to let her be my son."

My father gave a light laugh.

"That is your imagination."

"Not imagination. That is a fact. I really saw and heard it in my dream."

"And so, you are sure that you will give birth to a son."

"Of course, I am."

My father shrugged his shoulders.

"Let's wait and see."

"OK, let's wait and see."

Coincidently, I was born ten months later. It confirmed my mother's belief.

Sometimes I asked myself some questions. Why did my mother dream like that? What does that dream mean? Was I really my father's youngest aunt in my past life? Why did I reincarnate? I was conceived in my mother's womb six years after my youngest grandma's death. So what was she before I was conceived in mother's womb? We have no eyes to see our past lives. We have no eyes to see our future lives. We don't know what happened to us before our existence. We don't know what will happen to us after our death.

And she thought that I am the reincarnation of my youngest grandma. Coincidently, when I started to speak (I started to talk at age six, at the same age when my youngest grandma started to talk), I called my dad 'Little Brother' like my youngest grandma called him. And so they confirmed that I was her reincarnation. Though I called my father 'Little Brother', I did not remember anything about my past life. I don't remember anything about my youngest grandma. Even though I was not the reincarnation of my father's youngest aunt, surely I must be the reincarnation of someone else. I believe in reincarnation. I believe in the theory of the cycle of death and rebirth. I believe in kammic forces. Maybe it is because I was born and grew up in the Buddhist culture. Maybe it is because I was born into a Buddhist family. So to speak, I was not born as a Buddhist. I was born just as a human being. My family, society, culture etc. shaped me into a Buddhist. There is a hidden cause. Why I was born into a Buddhist family, into a Buddhist culture, into a Buddhist society? What if I was born into a non-Buddhist family? What if I grew up in non-Buddhist culture and society?

Now let's go back to the story of the young woman. She was deserted by her lover, who lived together with her for two years. Even though she did not commit any mistake, she was mistreated and tortured mentally by her lover. She did her best. Later, she came to loath the relationship between man and woman called 'love'. Once she was a timid girl. But now she was a brave, self-possessed young woman. Her life style changed. Her mind set changed. Her personality changed. Her view of life changed.

If I tell her all these things, how will she respond? I can't imagine. Will she pretend that it is the story of someone else's, not of hers? Or will she tell me that it is the story in my mind and not the real one?

She remains silent.

Why does she say nothing now? Is it because she has nothing more to say? I have a different opinion. I believe that she has many questions to ask me. No doubt. She is a skillful interviewer and good speaker. She has good questions. She never tortured her interviewee with her questions. Her questions always carry outlets. This is not the first time I am being interviewed by her. No. This is the first time. Why do I presume that this is not the first time I am interviewed by her?

"You can skip this issue if you are not prepared," she says.

It is after I have been asked a question that she says this word. The question is about a crucial issue.

I am sure that this question is not what she asks, because I am sure that she is not such a stupid young woman who would ask such a silly question. Anyway, the question is buzzing in my head and I can't drive it out. It is strange that I can't drive the thing in my head out as I want. This suggests that I have no power over my own mind or that I am being disobeyed by my own mind. Or it seems that my mind is no longer my mind. I feel depressed. I remember a piece of verse I came across in a book of dhamma: *Mind is the forerunner of all mental states*. I see well what it means, because I have already read a detailed explanation about it in the same book. I use the phrase 'in the same book'. However, I have no memory of the title of the book. I have a bad memory for titles and names. If I recall correctly, it is one of many books on my bookshelves, not the book I borrowed from the library I always go to. The library I always go to has no such books.

I have six bookshelves, which signifies that I am a voracious reader and have a good knowledge of things. Strangely, I don't feel that I am such a person. Maybe I am a bookworm. I don't read books to take wisdom from them but to take intellectual pleasure from them. I enjoy words. I enjoy prose. I enjoy writing.

I have some boyhood and childhood friends and I can visualize some of their figures, features, ways of speaking etc. I never forgot the way they behaved. Their characters, their attitude etc. are still vivid in my memory, but I can't recollect some of their names. That is the greatest weakness of mine. When a boyhood friend greets me, the best thing I can do is squeeze his hand tightly as a sign that I know who and what he is. It is just covering my weakness. In my memory, I have no information about his identity. He is my friend. That is all I know about him. I know him well, yet I forget his name. That is too bad. This is a type of an insult to him. What can I do for having no good memory for names?

I have much interest in mind and in the study of mind. I am always curious about what other people are wondering. I want to enter other people's mind and investigate their thoughts. A short story about a young man (I call him Mind-Reader) who attempts to see things in the other people's mind occurs to me. I sense that it might be my short story. The problem is that I am not a short story writer and that my memory informs me that I never wrote a short story. The fact that it is my short story is unreasonable. We should not put aside the fact that the things we consider to be unreasonable happen in the world. It seems that my memory tells me something false. It is impossible that memory always tells the truth.

OK. Let's go back to the short story.

The story begins with, *Mind-Reader started to enter the man's mind* and ends with, *It was the first and the last time that Mind-Reader entered the other's mind*. Mind-Reader was alarmed when he saw the things in the mind of a man he admires and adores much. He thought that the man was very good and kind-hearted, because the man was very good and very kind-hearted. But what he saw in the man's mind was different from the real image of the man outside. The man was a fraud. The man was a murderer. The man was a rapist. Mind-Reader could not decide whether he should tell others what he saw in the man's mind or he should keep it secret. He felt that he should tell the truth as he saw. At the same time, he felt that telling the truth would not have favorable consequences. He also feared that his silence would put the others into danger.

I, like Mind-Reader in my short story, also want to read other people's mind. And when I was young, I imagined that I had such a psychic power of reading other people's mind. But now I don't want to have such a psychic power. I don't want to be a mind-reader any more.

My mind returns to the question. Is it important to me? Is it helpful to me? Is this dangerous to me? Or is it a reminder of what happened to me? There is no reason for me to forget what happened to me. Everything is clear in my mind. I have no damage in my head, in my brain. However I can't figure out why I am sitting here in a large room.

Questions play a crucial role in developing one's thinking power. Questions can enlighten one's mind. But some questions make no sense and have no use. They do the business of torturing the mind only.

Maybe someone asked me some questions recently, or maybe I ask myself some questions just now. Memory is not reliable. It is like a box in which different sorts of things are crammed. Things in it are distorted, deformed, damage, and crushed beyond recognition. Who can say that everything we remember is as real as it happened? Maybe we remember things as we want, not as they really happened. Maybe what really happened to you is A, but what you remember is B. However I believe that I have a good memory. Is that true? Maybe even that belief is false.

My memory tells me that I had a friend, who had to quit school at nine or ten. It was in the third standard that he left school. At that time, I had no idea why he stopped learning. However, later I came to realize why, which broke my heart.

He had curly hair and a round face. He spoke so fast that some could not get what he said, and when other people could not follow what he said, I had to serve as his interpreter. He looked like his father. His mother was a good speaker, who had many good stories to share.

When we were young, she told us stories. Most of the stories she told me were fable-like. I do not know how she got the stories. I never asked her about it. She could not read, so it is certain that it is not from books that she got the stories. I had no interest in how she got the stories. I was only interested in how she told her stories. She told me the fable-like stories and I liked all. To me that's perfect. I needed nothing more. I remember all the stories she told me and my friend. Till now I like her stories. The problem is that my memory failed to keep their appearances, features and figures. So I can't visualize them well. They are like phantoms. But I am sure that the stories she told us were real.

For that, my memory seems to be responsible. And I can't help asking some questions. Is memory reliable? Are you sure what you really remember is what you really experienced? Maybe what you really experienced is A and what you really remember is B. Can you guarantee that your memory kept things as they really happened to you or as it wanted?

I glance at the young woman in the grey uniform to check the expression on her face. She is not looking at me now. Instead, she is reading something or pretending to read something on her laptop screen. So I don't see her expression and fail to check. Anyway, I can say that she has some more questions to ask me. I cannot say what they are. I hope they might be the ones I can answer. Surprisingly or fortunately, I could answer everything she had asked.

Now questions occur to me. Why do I have ready-made answers to her questions? Have I read all questions and answers by heart? Why? Is this a scene of a film?

I have no idea how many times I have already asked myself these damn questions. I don't want to find myself in this mess, but I can't find a way to escape from this. What or who did throw me into this mess?

Complete silence in the room. No sound, no voice but those of my words in my mind. What does this silence denote? A threat? A danger? Peace? Time to escape? The end? Or something? Silence is so long that I can't bear it any longer. I want someone to break the silence. I want someone to speak something. No one speaks. Everyone is lifeless. FUCK IT!

A thought stirs in me, and I decide to explain something to her. I hope she will not cut me off in mid explanation.

Chapter V
In the Long Silence

The long heavy silence ends as successfully as I have expected. It is not because someone starts to speak, but because someone drops a glass onto the concrete floor, making a very loud noise. Everyone is alarmed to hear the loud noise. But I am pleased to hear it. And I thank the person who has dropped the glass. It does not matter whether he dropped it intentionally or unintentionally. What matters is that he has dropped it successfully. Now I feel relaxed and comfortable.

I hope for the following successive noises created by rebuking, blaming, pleading, as well.

Someone superior will rebuke: the others will blame: the person who dropped the glass will plead. But none of these things happens as I hoped. No one rebukes. No one blames. No one pleads. And so no noise.

Now the duty to break the silence falls on me, I suppose. "What should I say?" is the question which enters my mind first. This does not help.

Before I can utter anything, the first interviewer breaks the silence in a skillful way. "Do you believe a word, a line or a book can change someone's view of life?"

"Yes, I do," I reply unhesitatingly. I believe in this theory. But I have a view that this theory may not be right one hundred percent. It may be right only for those with a special brain. It may not be right for an idiotic person like me. I have read about a few great men whose lives changed after reading a word, a line or a book.

I pause for a few seconds for thoughts and add: "Nietzsche confessed that reading Schopenhauer's *The World as Will and*

Representation turned him into a philosopher. That's true. But some might presume that it is not true."

She remains silent, making no comment. She knows about Nietzsche no less than I do. We talk about Nietzsche occasionally when the subject of our conversation is about the misconception of a philosopher's words. Some time ago she gave a remark, "Schopenhauer's *The World as Will and Representation* changed Nietzsche into a philosopher. But it could not change the other readers into philosophers, I suppose. I might be wrong." At that time, I said that I had the same view.

"Thank you for telling me about Nietzsche," she says, as if she has no knowledge of Nietzsche. She has already read Nietzsche's *Thus Spoke Zarathustra* three or four times. It is obvious that she is hiding reality.

I study her eyes, which show no sign that she feels guilty about anything. I am perplexed.

"My pleasure," I reply. What I really want to say is, 'Why are you pretending not to know about Nietzsche?', yet realizing that it will embarrass her, I chose to say politely, "Is there a word, a line or a book that changed your life?"

A good question. A difficult answer.

Any word, any line or any book I have read could not change my life. I am rather idiotic. It is a very rare thing that a word, a line or a book can change one's life. It demands several reasons and facts. It may be a very hard thing for an idiotic person like me. This theory may be right only for a few people with a special talent and a high personality.

"I am sorry," I say. "My memory is not enough good to remember such things." I am not sure whether what I have said is relevant or not.

She smiles. "OK. No problem," she writes something on the laptop for a few seconds. "I also have no memory of a book which changed my life." Her tone of voice and expression on her face reveal that she is telling the truth.

I am glad to hear that she is the same as me. That she does not remember which book changed her life is the truth. That fear changed her life is the truth. That she does not dare to admit it is the truth. What's more, that we live with fears is truth, too. I wonder if I should tell her these things. I don't want to irritate her with these words. I just want to wake her up from fear and from false identity. In truth, I have no right to say 'false identity', because it is impossible to say which identity is real and which identity is false. The truth is that identity is identity.

Judging from her expression, I am certain she is determined to do something. Something, I don't know exactly what it is. My instinct cautions me that it is not good for me. I have no option. Do we have options in our lives? Do we choose something we like or do we try to like something we get? What was the option in my early life? What is the option in my life now?

"What do you think about this conversation?" This is the question the young woman in the blue uniform asks. She is the fourth interviewer.

While I am thinking about the answer to her question, my mind flies towards the past.

When I was a middle school student, my female teacher asked all students in the class about their dreams or the aims in their lives. And my turn came.

"What do you want to be?" my teacher asked.

"Nothing, Sayarma," I answered.

Almost every student laughed at my answer. However, a student did not laugh. He even praised me, instead. He was my friend, who was good at telling stories. (I have told you about this in the previous chapter, but I forgot to tell you something relevant.)

I had no intention to insult them. But they felt that they were insulted. What I really meant was one thing and what they interpreted was the other. They misunderstood my words. Misconception was the cause of misinterpretation, which made them feel insulted. They laughed at me in class. That was not a problem. The problem was that they saw me as an enemy later. I tried to explain, but it did not help. The result was that we never became friends.

"Sometimes, what we say simply happens to insult others," the fourth interviewer comments. "We feel sorry for this, but we have no guilty conscience, because we know well that what we say it not on purpose."

I give her a quick, surprised look. How does she know the things I am thinking? Is she a mind-reader?

When I am about to ask her something about her mind-reading, she reminds me, "I hope you don't forget that I asked you a question."

"No, I haven't," I reply.

I don't know what to say. To be honest, I don't like this conversation. Anyway, I should not say as I feel. I should say something good. I must avoid any word which may insult her.

"A conversation is necessary for actors and actresses," I say.

She shrugs her shoulders. "You do not think that I put the determiner 'this' before the word 'conversation' unintentionally, do you?"

She may have other reasons to say this, but it surely amuses me.

"Oh, yes. *This* conversation helps me a lot," I say, emphasizing the determiner 'this'. Unexpectedly my word uncovers the thing I failed to notice. I feel excited.

Her eyes widen in surprise. I know that she is faking. "Really?" she asks with feigned surprise.

I can't help smiling. "Of course," I reply emphatically, "some questions remind me to reflect on my experience. Some questions remind me to meditate on the importance of being."

Judging from the expression on her face, I can say that she is satisfied with my answer.

And I feel at ease. I tell her as I really feel and think. Sometimes we fail to reflect on the things we should reflect upon. Unless an event or a question reminds us, we will never reflect on such things. In this conversation, some questions are great help to me. I can't imagine why the idea to say how I feel and think does not occur to me.

"In reality, I should say thanks to you all," I say solemnly.

"For what?" she asks, as if not knowing what I mean.

"For this conversation."

The interviewers exchange glances.

I notice the amused expression on their faces.

In my mind, I say, *I should make myself prepared.* Here the question is: *what for?* It is impossible to predict what is going to happen in the coming seconds. It is hard to see for what I must prepare myself. I must wait. I must watch. I should not be afraid of anything. I should not let fear enter my mind.

What can I...

Before I can finish my sentence in my mind, my mind reminds me. Now it is not time to ask myself what I can do. Now it is time to make myself ready for everything.

The young woman in the blue uniform is writing something. The room is so silent that I can hear her pressing the keys on her laptop. It produces a rhythmic sound. To my ears, it is very pleasant to hear.

She goes on typing rhythmically. He said that he is satisfied with his career as an actor. When I asked him about his love affair, his answer is complicated. He did not give an exact answer. I asked the other indirect question about his love affair. Amazingly, he could shun the questions well. He wants to know if I am a mind-reader or not.

She did not ask me about my love affair. She did not ask me the question whether I am satisfied with my career as an actor. Everything except the final comment—HE WANTS TO KNOW IF I AM A MIND-READER OR NOT—is false. Why does she write false facts? The public will take these as the truth. I see that I should stop her. But I fail to say something. My mouth can't produce any voice. I see that I should make the gesture of stopping. But I fail to move my hands, my eyes and my eyebrows. My limbs are being controlled. I can't do anything but to give up. To give up is to surrender. To surrender is the sign of loser. Am I a loser? I never wanted to be a loser. I am, however, a loser now. This is reality. It is impossible to avoid this reality. This reality, like any other reality, is hard to accept.

Who says I am a loser? I must encourage myself. I must cry out loudly: I CAN DO IT. There is always the way. Your duty is to find out. To do this, you must have great will. It will be totally wrong if you take me as the type of person who gives up easily.

Without any reason, I am curious to know what time it is now. And I look at my watch, hopefully. I notice that its hands do not move at all. The hands show that the watch stopped at quarter to nine. I lose my hope. Now is it quarter to nine? It is impossible. If it is not quarter to nine, what time is it now?

No problem. I have my cell phone. It can tell me what time it is. I take out my cell phone. Then I switch it on. I can't switch it on. Its battery is flat. Is this a coincidence? I don't think so. If not, what can it be? A plot? A misfortune?

I wonder about why I want to know what time it is now. To know or not to know time is nothing to me. There must be a reason for this curiosity. I seem to have the misconception that knowing what time it is now can provide a clue to what is happening to me.

I look at the fourth interviewer's left wrist. I see no watch on her left wrist or right wrist. Surely I saw it a few minutes ago, that was not an illusion. Maybe she took off the watch.

"Can I ask you something," I ask in a very polite tone of voice.

She nods affirmatively. "Of course, you can." Her manner shows that she is in a good mood.

I had hardly seen her in a bad mood. Maybe that's why she has a good practice of keeping mind calm. I can't help admiring her.

Though she shows no sign of recognizing me, I recognize her well. I don't recall when, where, and how we started to know each other (In fact, it is not correct to say *we started to know each other*, because though I know her, she does not know me. Therefore, I should say *I started to know her*, instead), but I know not only who and what she is now but what happened to her in her girlhood.

Her girlhood was filled with various kinds of hardships. She had no good friends to confide. Fortunately, she found writing her outlet, and she wrote down her feelings on blank sheets of papers. She is a good journalist and a writer, as well. She told me once that she has no memory of when and how she started to fall into the habit.

"I was very fortunate," she narrated. "My sorrows, grievances, indignations etc. turned into writings. And I did not meet with severe repression. And I did not suffer acute trauma much."

She had to encounter a series of emotional blows of life in her girlhood. But they did not have a chance to assault her, because she turned nearly all emotional blows into writings. It is a great gift. She couldn't imagine how she got it, or when she got it. In her grandfather's generation or in her parents' generation, there was no one who had such a gift. Fortunately, she was born with this gift. Without this gift, it would be very hard for her to avoid trauma and its symptoms, because the blows of her life were so heavy.

I remember that she told me that she was rewriting her three novels. When I look at her to tell about what she told me, she avoids my eyes.

I want to know what is in her mind. Is she thinking about her novels or about her girlhood or about what will happen to her next? We spend most of our time, thinking about something. We think about the past. We think about the future. We hardly think about the present, because the present is what we can't think about. The present is so swift that it is gone before we can think about it.

Though I can't recollect when and where we talked about her novels, I recollect well the things we conversed about.

At that time, she had published her first novel. In it, she spotlights the invisible threat to our society.

"Now I am rewriting my second novel. I hope I will finish it next month," she said.

"Do you always rewrite your stories?" I asked.

"Yes, I always do."

"How many times?"

"At least three or four times."

"How many times have you rewritten your second novel?"

"Five times."

"Oh, you are very patient and very hardworking."

"You flattering me, aren't you?" she asked, with smile.

"No, no, no. I didn't flatter you. I am telling the truth."

"Now I am rewriting the last part of the last chapter."

"How many chapters does the novel have?"

"Nine."

"Is it a big book?"

"Maybe. I will send a soft copy of the novel to you via email."

"Thank you. I am sure it is an interesting novel," I encouraged.

She shrugged, "Sorry, I can't guarantee that my novel will bring pleasure to you, because I don't write novels for pleasure."

"I don't seek pleasure in novels."

"What do you seek?"

"Nothing."

"Oh, what a coincidence!" she exclaimed. "It is the same for me: I don't hunt for anything in a novel," she gave no reason. Similarly, she did not ask me the reason.

Now I need to know what time it is. However, I don't want to ask her what time it is now. So I ask her another question, instead.

"How many novels have you written?"

She lifts her eyebrows.

"Sorry, I never wrote any novel," she replies.

In fact, I know beforehand what she will answer. Judging from the expression on her face, I can guess that she does not remember she has written a novel and is rewriting a second novel. If she can't recognize me, then she certainly will not recollect anything real.

I know she likes detective crime fictions and that she reads Edgar Allen Poe, Ross Macdonald, Craig Holden, and James Hall. And I want to test her whether she has memory of reading those writers.

"You read detective fictions a lot, don't you?" I ask.

She gives me a surprised look.

"Yes, I do. I read Edgar Allen Poe, Ross Macdonald, Craig Holden, and James Hall," she answers. Then she looks at me and asks, "By the way, how do you know this?"

I don't know what to answer. In reality, I have no idea of how I know. I am not sure whether she told me or not.

"You told me, I think."

She lifts her eyebrows. "That's impossible."

"Okay, that's impossible. You did not tell me. This is just what I guessed."

"You can guess the exact writers I read. Are there other things you know about me?"

"I know you read a lot."

She nods. "You are right. I read a lot."

She reads something on her laptop, and says: "I inherited the reading habit from my mother. She is not only an avid reader but a good buyer of books. She bought some books two days ago. One of them is a classic novel written by Burma's famous novelist. Some books are no longer available in the book market now."

She is telling lies. It is not from her mother that she inherits the reading habit. Her mother is not an avid reader. Her mother is not a good buyer of books. And her mother did not buy any book two days ago. Everything she tells me is a lie. How do I know this? It is very simple. She herself, she told me all these things. Her mother has no interest in reading. Her mother never bought a book. Even when she bought books, her mother blamed and scolded her. I should not let her know that I know that she is telling lies. I must pretend that I believe in what she is telling me. It is hard to pretend to believe something without believing it. It is hard to pretend not to know something while knowing it.

She has already told me that her mother was too lazy to read. Now she tells me that she inherits the reading habit from her mother. Which is true? She told me that her mother died of cancer three years ago. Now she tells me that her mother bought some books two days ago. Which is true?

If that her mother died of cancer three years ago is true, then that her mother bought some books two days ago must be untrue. If that her mother bought her some books two days ago is true, then that her mother died of cancer three years ago must be untrue. If both facts are true, then her mother might have been resurrected. That the both facts are true, is impossible. If one is true, then the other must be false. One possibility is that she, while talking about reading and about books, forgets that her mother died of cancer. Another possibility is that her mother is alive and she thought her mother died. There are other possibilities, too.

Whether her mother is alive or dead does not matter. What matters now is the reason why she said such things. Something wrong in her memory? Something wrong in her morality? As far as I know, she has a good memory. As far as I know, she is a righteous young woman.

I can't remember who introduced me to her. Did I introduce myself to her? It is impossible, because I never did such a thing. But I remember well that there is a certain relationship between the two of us. She looks like a writer more than an interviewer. Do I know her as a writer or as an interviewer? I don't want to think about it now. I must rest first. My mind needs to rest, I suppose.

When I think about nothing, a story enters my mind or my mind enters a story.

A man of about thirty finds himself in a taxi. He feels dizzy. He can't believe what he sees. He can't see anything clearly. He feels that everything he sees is covered by something like a fog. He is sure that his eyesight is not bad. Someone hit him on the head, and he has been unconscious for a few minutes. While he was unconscious, he was put into a taxi. Now he starts to regain consciousness. But the injury he received is so severe that he can't see things clearly. That's why he feels light-headed now. This is what he reflects on, what he experiences. And he puts his fingertips against his scalp. He hopes that he will find something like a bump or a gash, a swelling or a cut. He finds nothing. But he can't accept it. He can't believe it.

If he did not receive any severe injury on the head, then why does he feel dizzy, he ponders. And he asks himself why he finds no sign of injury on his head. He received injury on his head, yet the sign of injury disappeared before he regains consciousness, he supposes. Here the question is: how did it disappear? He gets no answer, which annoys him.

He is aware that he is well-dressed. His hair is neatly combed. This demonstrates that he was not attacked by anyone. He has no idea why he feels dizzy if he was not attacked. The only answer to all his question is: *no*. There is no other way to figure out reality. But he does not want to give up. He encourages himself that he will be able find the right answer at the right time.

He does not know to where the taxi is leading. And he asks the driver where they are going. The driver's answer surprises him. He has never heard the name of something the driver tells him. Maybe it is the name of a place or the name of a road. Maybe it is the name of a building, like condominium.

"Is it a place?"

"We can call it a place," he says, "OK, let's call it a place,"

"What kind of place is it?"

"A secret place where revolutionists meet," the driver says.

"Revolutionists? Who are they?"

"I am afraid I don't know, sir."

"Why are we going there?"

The driver's answer is simple and complicated. "I was told to take you there. That is why we are going there."

"Who told you?"

"Someone, sir."

"You mean you will not tell me who he is."

"My duty is just to take you there. Now I am serving my duty."

"Duty?"

"Yes, duty."

Their conversation pauses for a few minutes. The man is wondering about the secret place. He is trying to visualize, yet he fails. The picture of the place does not appear in his mind. This suggests that he has never been there. Besides, he presumes that he is not a revolutionist. He can't see himself as a revolutionist. If so, why he is going to the secret place where revolutionists gather. He can't imagine himself as a revolutionist. He has witnessed various strikes, but he did not take part in any strike. He is a coward. He does not have enough courage to be a revolutionist, he supposes.

So that might be a lie. They are not leading to a secret place where revolutionists always meet. They are leading somewhere else.

He remembers the driver's words: *I am serving my duty*. He sympathizes with the driver, who feels obligated to bring him somewhere. Now he suspects that he is being taken to the police station. But he is not in handcuffs. He is sure that he never committed any crime. He is sure that he is not a criminal. He believes in his morality. If he is taken to the police station as a criminal, he must be in handcuffs. This thought makes him feel better.

"Do you know about me?" he asks.

The driver shakes his head and replies: "No, sir."

This is not what he hoped from the driver, and he feels bewildered. To his astonishment, he does not feel scared. But he feels that he is going to experience something unusual. He can't predict what it might be, good or bad. He is curious about his future now. He was never curious about his future. He has encountered various hardships, misfortunes, and troubles. So it can be said that he is an experienced person. Whatever will happen to him, he will surely be able to handle it.

"You told me that you don't know me. How could you distinguish me from others?"

"They told me to take you, so I took you. That is all I know."

"Where did you pick me up from?"

"At the north gate of the City Park: they told me to pick you up from there."

He sees the City Park in his mind. It is hard for him to believe it. He hardly goes to the park, even once a year. Whenever he makes an appointment with someone, he always choses a café. He can't figure out the reason why he went to the park. He can't imagine what cajoled him to go there.

"How did you know that I am the one they told you to pick up?"

"Maybe my instinct told me," the driver says, with a confident smile on his face.

"Have you ever met those fellows personally?"

"No, sir. It is on phone that they always order me to do things."

"Now they are waiting for us at the secret place."

"Not at the secret place. They are waiting for you somewhere else. My duty is to drop you at the secret place."

"How many people have you brought to them?"

"By dozens, sir."

"Do you know what happened to those?"

The driver shakes his head. "I was warned that I must keep my nose out of their business."

He sighs and studies the driver, who remains calm.

"Don't feel remorse for what you have done?"

The driver is surprised at his words. "Why do I? I served my duty. And now I am serving my duty."

"What if what you do is criminal?"

"Why do you say that?"

"Because you took me without my knowledge, without my consent. And surely you did the same thing to others."

"No, no, sir. I brought you with your knowledge, with your consent," the driver explains. "Before I picked you up, I explained everything to you."

"You explained to me?"

"Of course, I did."

"Then?"

"Then you got into my car."

"Without any word, without any negative response?"

The driver nods and replies: "Exactly."

He feels that the driver's voice is louder than necessary.

"I was unconscious for some minutes. When I recovered consciousness, I found myself in your car. So it is impossible that I got into your car with my knowledge, with my consent."

"So do you presume that I knocked you unconscious before I put you into my car?" the driver asks.

He nods and replies: "Exactly." His tone of voice confirms that he is so much confident of what he has said.

The driver shrugs his shoulders. "You know, the City Park is a very busy place. If I knocked you unconscious, then the others in the park would surely see it. They would attack me to save you. I would surely be arrested. Do you think they would neglect you?" the driver pauses to think about something. He cannot see what is in the driver's mind. He does not want to read the driver's mind. A few minutes later, the driver adds, "What's more, you see, you are stout. I am skinny and weak. You are much stronger than me. It will be reasonable to say that you knocked me unconscious or you overpowered me. How could I overpower you? How could I knock you unconscious? Even if I could do it in some ways, how could I put your heavy body into my car? How could I lift and carry your body? You agreed. So I took you. Why is this criminal?"

The driver's words are reasonable. However, he senses that something is missing in the driver's words. Beginning of the story is missing. What happened to him before he found himself in the car was hidden or lost. It is a very important part of the story. It is a link. It is a clue. According to the driver's words, he must be in the park. The driver came to him and asked him. And he got into the car. He supposes that all these things should be in his memory if all these things really happened to him.

Though he senses that something is missing, he can't figure it out. He has tried all possible ways of logical reasoning.

"Let it be. But drop me over there."

"Sorry, sir. I must bring you to the secret place."

"Why?"

"It is my duty. I never fail to perform my duty."

"What if I bully you to do so?"

"I believe that you will never do it. You never bullied anyone."

He never bullied anyone. He is a very kind-hearted person. How does the driver know this?

His mind leaves the present moment without his consent. He has no idea when his mind flew.

It was yesterday. He was at the birthday party of a young woman, the librarian of their company. The party started at seven o'clock. He is sure that he was not drunk at the party. At about ten o'clock, they parted. He took a taxi to his apartment. He can remember everything he encountered and did yesterday night. He did nothing wrong. No one did anything wrong. Nothing wrong happened. Nothing wrong he detected. Nothing bad he encountered. He suspects that there is something he fails to remember. He suspects that there was something he failed to notice at the party. The party started successfully. The party ended successfully. As far as he can remember, everything at the party was normal. Everyone was happy at the party. Everyone enjoyed the party. Certainly, everyone had a very good day.

At the party, some talked about their jobs. At the party, some talked about their childhood. At the party, some talked about everything. At the party, some talked about nothing. At the party, some tried to flee from the miseries for a short moment. He can't remember what he talked about. Perhaps he, like a speech impaired one, remained silent.

Yesterday he might be a little drunk, and went to bed late. Today morning, he woke up to a noise. He can't remember when she gets up from the bed. Usually he gets up from the bed at six o'clock. The clock on the wall warned him that it was nine o'clock. He never woke up very late. This was the first time he woke up late, which surprised him very much.

The party was held on Friday night, so he got up on Saturday morning. On Friday night, he was drunk and went to bed, feeling faint. The result was that he forgot the usual time to get out of bed. And so he rose very late the next morning. Feeling dizzy now might be because he drank too much last night. Usually he does not drink much. Whenever he drinks too much, he feels dizzy when he gets up from bed. He, therefore, always puts a limitation on drinking. It seems that on the Friday night, he failed to remind himself about the limitation he himself imposed. Was it the first cause of this misfortune?

There is no doubt that he can remember well that he got up from bed in the morning. The problem is that what happened to him after waking up is not in his memory. He was drunk at the party yesterday. It was Friday night. He woke up on Saturday morning, feeling dizzy. Seemingly, his memory did not record any events which happened after nine o'clock in the morning: the last thing he can recall was that he woke up at nine. After nine, what did happen to him? What did happen to him on Saturday afternoon? What did happen to him on Saturday evening? He does not know what time it is now, yet he knows well that it is evening. However, he is not sure whether this is Saturday evening or Sunday evening, Monday evening or Tuesday?

If this is Sunday evening, one day's events are missing. If this is Monday evening, two days' events are missing. If this is Tuesday evening, three days' events are missing. He calculates that there must be a close relationship between what is happening to him and the missing days. He is confident that if he can uncover this relationship, everything will become clear. He needs someone's help to do this. It is impossible to get help from someone now. He is in a taxi, and no one he can trust is with him. He is alone. He is helpless. He is the only one who can help him. He is the only one he can trust.

He surmises that he can defeat the driver easily. But he does not want to attack anyone now. Strangely, he sympathizes with the driver's duty. In his view, the driver is performing his duty, doing as ordered. He driver has no right or power to say no to his duty. And he asks himself what his duty is. Is his duty to surrender himself to fate? Is this what destiny has planned for him? He has no faith in destiny. He, however, feels indignant and questions his faith by the time he comes to realize that he has no choice but to surrender. Why does he have no options?

"Do you know that I work at a book publishing company," he asks the driver, with the hope that he will get the right answer.

"I am sorry, sir," the driver replies, turning the car into the one-way street. "I don't know what your job is."

He feels depressed, because what he hears from the driver differs what he hoped to hear. "I think I am an editor of a publishing house. What do you think?"

"My answer is the same: I don't know, sir."

He sighs. He does not want to blame the driver for all this.

"I am terribly sorry," the driver apologizes. "In fact, I should know about you a little so that I can tell you what you are when you ask me."

"Are you joking?"

"No, no. Not joking, sir."

"I am sure that I am an editor," he says, with a confident expression on his face. "I just asked you because I wanted to check whether you have knowledge about me."

The driver stays silent. Who knows what is in his mind?

He tries to think about the books he has edited. Some titles of the books intrude his mind. All titles are amazing. He feels doubt as to whether they are the books which he has edited or which he has read as a general reader. In spite of the fact that he can't confirm his editorship, he can confirm that all books are novels. Although the titles of the books are in his memory, his memory does not keep the names of their writers.

In his mind, he sees a man who decides which novel should be published and which novel should not be published. He tries to find out the man's name, but he fails. Ten names occur in his mind. None of them is the man's name, he feels. And so he tries again. He is the type of person who keeps trying to find out the answer until he gets it finally.

"Was I destined to be an editor?"

He had no wish to ask this question aloud.

The driver hears his question and turns towards him. "That's a question I also ask myself sometimes."

"And what is the answer?" he asks eagerly, with the hope that he will learn something from the driver. The driver does not add anything. And silence intervenes.

Only some minutes later, he breaks the silence. "Every question has an answer," he is aware that he says this with an I-know-everything tone of voice. "But we can't find it. It is not because questions have no answer. It is just because we can't go beyond the boundaries of our knowledge."

The driver seems to be baffled by these words.

Suddenly, my mind comes out of the story before it ends. I am not sure when the story will end. But I am sure that the story can attract my mind. The story puts many questions into my mind. I feel as if I am the man in the story. In fact, it is impossible.

All people in the room are busy. They are all dutiful workers. The young woman does not ask me any questions now. She is busy typing. She has no time to have a conversation with me. Great! I have time to take rest. Sometimes I notice her speaking with the other young women, who are also busy typing. It seems that they are all writing essays based on what we have talked about. I have no doubt that they will not neglect what they have heard. I really trust their morality, personality, and ability. I, however, fear that they will write what I did not tell them.

"I hope you do not write what I did not say."

My words stop them from typing. They all look at me and utter something in unison, which marks their fit of pique.

At once I realize that I have done something wrong. It is too late to take my deed back. All I can do now is apologize to all of them. What a good idea!

"I am terribly sorry," I apologize. "I didn't mean to offend you."

"We see," one of the young women says, in monotone.

See *what*? Her word carries ambiguity. Her tone carries annoyance. I try to decode it. But I fail.

Afterwards, I decide not to say anything. I must watch what they write. No matter whether what they write would differ from what I really have said. The readers will take what they write as the truth. If they write that my boyhood dream was to be an actor, the readers will see me as a very ambitious and persevering guy who can carry out his dream, and I will become their idol.

I never dreamt of being anyone's idol. I want to lead a quiet life. I want to lead a carefree life.

"Well, let's restart our conversation now," the young woman before me announces. Her tone of voice sounds commanding.

I don't like commands. I don't like to be ordered. To say *Yes, I do* or to say *No, I don't* is loathsome to me. If I do something, it is just because I want to do it, not because I am commanded to do it. If I do not do something, it is just because I don't want to do it, not because I am commanded not to do it.

Now I feel that the young woman commands me to restart our conversation. I don't like it at all. But I can't refuse her request. I must consent to her request.

"I think we should."

"You said that though you've starred in a few dozen films, only two of those films you liked best."

I did not say it like that. I, however, say yes now.

"What I would like to question is: what are the titles of those films?"

Titles of two films slip out of my mouth. I can't believe it.

"Those films did not meet with success. Can you tell me why?"

"I am not sure. But I think that it is because of wrong timing and wrong place."

"I remember that in an interview, you said that some were born in the wrong time and in the wrong place," she said.

I nod and say yes. "I don't remember when and where I said so."

"It does not matter. What I would like to know is: Do you use these phrases in the same sense here?"

"Exactly, in the same sense. My view remains the same. Even now I will repeat the same words. Sometimes I feel that I am among those who were born at the wrong time and in the wrong place."

"Is it a sign of depression?"

"No. Not at all. It is the sign of something else."

"You don't mean to say that you never suffered from depression, do you?"

"I admit that I suffered a lot from depression several times. To suffer from depression is not shameful. If you suffer from depression, it confirms that you are normal."

The young woman is satisfied with my answer, I guess. "That is why the other actors and actresses said that you are not only an actor but a free thinker."

"They said!" I exclaim.

"Surely, they said. Some of them idolize you."

"That's bad. I don't want to be idolized by anyone."

"Why?"

"If you're idolized by someone, then you are trapped. To me idolatry is a threat."

Certainly, it will be hard for her to accept what I have said. She is ready. She might presume that it must be a crazy guy who does not want to be idolized. Even she might like being idolized.

She shrugs her shoulders and says: "I have never seen a person who does not like being idolized. If I am right, everyone likes being idolized."

"Including you?"

She gives a light laugh. "Of course, including me," she says. "You know, I am normal, not like you." After saying so, she laughs heartily.

How she is laughing is very innocent. To laugh heartily is not easy. One must be free from anxiety, worries, and stress. I am not sure whether I can laugh like that, because I have anxiety, worries, and stress now. I must drive them out first.

Now she stops laughing. I see tears in her eyes. She closes her eyes. Then she wipes tears with a piece of tissue.

The other young women do not laugh with her. They smile and study me. What is in every young woman's mind is a puzzle to me.

"OK, let it be," the other young woman in the grey uniform says. "Can you tell me what drove you to dream to be an actor?"

"If I remember correctly, I did not tell anyone that I had a dream to be an actor. If you learnt it from someone, it is certain that he fooled you."

My words sound harsh and rude. But they reflect reality.

"So, there is nothing which drove you to dream to be an actor?"

I can't imagine why she asks me the same question to which I have given the same answer indirectly. She seems to be so stupid.

I feel disappointed. Anyway, I try to be patient.

"All of you asked the same questions again and again, and I gave the same answer again and again," I say. I notice my tone of voice is offensive. I understand that I should tone down my criticism, but I fail. "I think you should stop this game."

I can't imagine why I happened to us the word 'game'. In which sense I happened to use it, I have no idea.

I seemingly run out of patience now. I calm myself down. I should be patient. I should not behave like a teenage boy. I don't know how old I am. I am about thirty or forty. I say in my mind that perhaps I am about the young women's age. The problem is that I can't guess their age. Maybe they are about thirty or so. And am I? Perhaps I am older than or younger than them. If I have a mirror into which I can look, certainly I can guess my age, I suppose.

All the young women begged my pardon. And I also begged their pardon. They did something wrong to me. Similarly, I also did something wrong to them. I have no reason not to apologize them. I am responsible because of what I have said. I should choose words with attention.

I ask myself why I am ashamed of having a dream or of being asked about my dream. Am I sure that I had no dream? To have a dream or to have no dream is the same.

I try to see it from other angles:

I had a dream and I forgot it.

The reality that I had a dream was deleted.

I had a dream and I don't dare to confess it.

I had a dream and my memory was ruined so that I can't remember it.

"Terribly sorry, maybe I forgot that I had a dream," I apologize. "What's more I should not speak like that. I have no idea why I failed to control my temper. I have no idea why I was in a bad mood."

All of them say nothing. They look at each other. I can't guess what they are discussing, by means of eye contact.

"I am not giving reasons," I say.

They stay silent. The whole room is silent at that moment, which seems to threaten me. I want to liberate myself out of this dreadful silence.

I study them. I see no trace of indignation on their faces. What a huge relief!

"We all know that you are not such an aggressive type," one of the young women says.

The others support her word, with the same expression on their faces.

"Thank you."

"For what?"

"For your forgiveness."

"Oh, great! And we all thank you for your THANK YOU."

We all laugh in unison.

I have no idea why I laugh. I have no reason not to laugh.

"Should we talk about your future plan? What do you think?" asks the young woman in the blue uniform.

"Well, let's talk about my future plan."

"Rumor has it that this film is the last one in which you will appear and that you will no longer act."

I shrug my shoulders. "I have also heard the rumor."

"So?"

"So, rumor is rumor is rumor."

"Do you mean that you have no thought of leaving the world of film?"

"What I can say at this moment is that this is not the last film I will act in."

"By the way, can I ask you about your marriage, sir?"

The other young woman's question makes me think about a young woman. She is young. She is beautiful. She is brave. This is all I know about her.

"We heard that you will marry a beautiful young woman this year. Is it just a rumor, sir?"

I think, I shake my head. This suggests that what they heard is not a rumor. If it is not a rumor, then surely it must be true. And if it is true, then my marriage will be held this year.

I have told no one about my marriage. I have told no one about my love affair. Even my confidantes do not know that I fell in love with a beautiful young woman. I did not let them know about my lover. It is not because I want to keep my love affair secret, just because I feel that it is not the time to tell the truth. I don't like to keep the truth secret, but sometimes we have to keep the truth secret when it is not the time to uncover the truth.

"May I know your view on love and marriage?"

"I suppose I know what love is and what marriage is. But I don't know how to explain to you."

"Do you think that your life will become better after your marriage?"

"How can I say that? Now I am single, not a married man."

"Are you not sure?"

"Even if I am sure, I will not let you know about it."

"Why?"

"I want you to try to detect."

"Now I can trace something."

"Something? You don't know what it is. Do you?"

"No, sir."

"Good."

"Sometimes even a very simple question demands a very painstaking effort to get an answer."

"I see now," says the young woman in the red uniform. I see the letters MSTV on her uniform. MSTV is a popular channel. It is famous for its interview program.

What does she see now? Now my mind is incredibly calm. I see things clearly. Probably this is the first time that I am in a good mood and trust what I experience. I look around the room. Everyone is working. They are all dutiful, burying their minds in the work. I guess that our conversation might be very important.

"Can you tell me about *Mr. Driver*?" the young woman in the pink uniform asks. Her tone of voice expresses that she is a little excited. I don't know what the reason is. Maybe it is because she fears that I will refuse.

"Of course, I can. *Mr. Driver* is not a smash."

"But you did your best as Mr. Driver in *Mr. Driver*."

"No doubt, I did my best," I say. "By the way, why do you want to know about the film which did not meet with success?"

"Sorry, I don't know why. But I am sure that I want to know about it."

"Let's start with the story of Mr. Driver," I say. I am not sure whether the story can attract her. "In truth, he has a name given by his parents, but people forget his real name and call him Mr. Driver. He leads a simple life, but he is not a simple-minded person. He is intelligent."

"I have never seen such guys," she says.

"He is not aggressive. Since his childhood he did not compete with other children. He never entered in any competition. Most of his friends wanted to be first in school. However, he never wanted to be first. His parents wanted him to be first in his school. He was too lazy to try to be first. Everyone, including his parents and friends knew well that if he wanted to be first, he would try to be first. He was very intelligent and had a good memory. So his parents wanted him to try to be first.

"My parents also wanted me to be first when I was young. When I did not get first prize, they scolded me. Especially my mother was angry with me, because I did not try to won first prize, and she beat me on the back."

"That's bad. My parents never told me to try to be first. They always told me to do my best."

"You are very lucky. I wish I want to be born with such parents."

"We have no option for our birth. Sometimes I ask myself why we have no right to choose parents, situation, place etc. Our birth, as you know, determines very important factors of our identity and our personality. The important factors such as hereditary, gene, and DNA are directly related to birth."

"OK. Let's go back to the story of Mr. Driver. He is always happy. He helps others. He likes being called Mr. Driver. His parents wanted to see him as an engineer, as a doctor, as a teacher etc. As for him, he loves driving. He becomes a driver. He never felt depressed or inferior being a driver."

"My uncle is also a taxi driver. He does not love driving. He does not like being called Mr. Driver. He wants others to call by his name. When he was young, he wanted to be an airline pilot. The problem was his poor eyesight. Although he gave up his great dream to be an airline pilot, his dream did not disappear. He collects toy planes."

"Your uncle lives with his dream. It seems that he can't accept reality."

"I think so."

"That is bad. Our Mr. Driver is not such a man. He lives life. He enjoys life. He has no dreams. He has no future plans. He sees life as life, not as a dream or not as something else."

She shrugs her shoulders and concludes: "Maybe he is mad."

"That is what your imagination makes you see him as, not what you see him as. Your imagination is the product of what you've learnt from schools or from society."

"Sorry, I disagree."

"I will not ask you to agree with me. I agree that you disagree."

She smiles. I don't want to define her smile, because I cannot guarantee that I can define it correctly. Surely I will define it, based on my imagination, not on what it really is.

Mr. Driver is mad as she concluded. And that madness is normal. The problem is the orthodox view of our society. Our society does not accept such type of madness. I must choose the right words to tell her about it. Even my words can be regarded as a threat to society. I am not a philosopher: I have no intention to threat the way of other peoples' life and uncertain future.

"In truth, we are trapped in the orthodox views of our society," I say. "Sometimes we call it *education*."

She looks at me with a surprised expression on her face. It is strange for her to hear such words from an actor. Perhaps, what she hopes to hear from me might be something else. She says nothing.

"We should not talk about the orthodox views of our society, I know."

I pause for a few moments and ask myself what I should talk about. I don't want to shock her. If I talk about the orthodox views of our society, she would surely be shocked. It is impossible for her to neglect such views, because she was molded by such education.

And I? No doubt that I was also molded by the same education. If so, how can I be free from its influence?

"We should mold ourselves. That is our right. That is our option," I say energetically.

She is silent. Her tired eyes confirm that she is baffled. "You are talking about Mr. Driver, aren't you?" she asks. She seems to think that our conversation deviates from its main subject.

"We didn't deviate from our main subject. I am talking about something related to *Mr. Driver*. I am talking about Mr. Driver."

"Sorry, I suppose that you are giving a philosophy lecture to me," she says, "and so I am about to tell you that I am not interested in philosophy." Her tone of voice suggests that she is kidding me.

I laugh. I am not sure whether I really want to laugh. I have told her that *Mr. Driver* is a boring film. She seems to forget it. Or I forgot to tell her that *Mr. Driver* is a boring film.

"*Mr. Driver* is a boring film. Two-thirds of the film is simply dialogues between Mr. Driver and his passengers or between two passengers," I say, but my mind is running around the thoughts of established laws and their influences on us.

Our society pays attention to the established laws more than necessary. Our society does not dare to revolt against such laws. I see that we are the prey of the established laws of our society. Most of the laws were born many years earlier before we were born. If we don't obey such laws, the thing we must face is our society. We are automatically becoming the enemy of the society. The way we think is a threat to our society. The way we live is a danger to our society. These severe accusations will be made against us. No way to escape.

"Can you tell me more about Mr. Driver and *Mr. Driver*?"

To her question, my mind jumps out of the thoughts.

"Surely, I can," I reply at once. I notice that she is impatient. I see it on her face easily. She is bad at hiding her emotions and feelings. Or I am good at detecting others' emotions and feelings.

"In fact, Mr. Driver is a guy who is not much influenced by the established laws of our society," I say. "He has no interest in the education that forces young generations into a fixed mold. He himself is the prey of such an education. What makes him different from others is that he has the strong will to be free and lives a free life." I pause and study her and the other young women. All of them are quiet. Their eyes are bright with passionate interest.

I thank myself for not forgetting about Mr. Driver.

"Mr. Driver is an alien, a stranger," concludes the young woman in the blue uniform. "He is very courageous, isn't he?"

"It is unquestionable. Not only that, he is righteous too."

"Wow! You are very lucky to act as Mr. Driver in *Mr. Driver*," exclaims the young woman in the pink uniform. Then she asks earnestly, "How did you feel when you learnt that you would star as Mr. Driver?"

"Rejoiced more than I can say."

To my words, all of them laugh hysterically. And I also join them.

"It was hard for me to be Mr. Driver," I confess when they all stop laughing. Then I continue. "I am not strong enough to rebel the orthodox educational system."

"So Mr. Driver is an imaginary type of a person, isn't he?" the young woman in the pink uniform asks. She seems to be dissatisfied with my words. "And do you mean that there is no one like Mr. Driver in the real world?"

"To be honest, sometimes I have doubts even in *real*, so I try to avoid this word as far as I can." My mind goes to the time when I read the stories of Socialist Realism in our country. "I must confess that I can't say yes or no. I can say that maybe there is a type of a person like Mr. Driver. I am not sure who he or she is. I am sure I am not that type of a person."

"And what about the story of *Mr. Driver*?"

"*Mr. Driver* begins with Mr. Driver driving in the morning and ends with Mr. Driver driving at night. In brief, the film is about Mr. Driver's one-day routine. It is also about Mr. Driver's life and philosophy. It is also about the passengers who get into his car. It is also about what is happening now in our country and in our world.

"The story goes chronologically, when Mr. Driver and his passengers are having conversations. But when Mr. Driver and his passengers talk about their past, the scenes are intercut.

"I have told you that *Mr. Driver* covers so many dialogues: dialogues between Mr. Driver and his passengers and dialogues amongst the passengers. Through dialogues, we can see what is happening in their lives, what is happening in our country, and what is happening in the world.

"Through flashback scenes, we can see what has happened to Mr. Driver and his passengers in the past. Those scenes help us understand them more.

"Really, *Mr. Driver* is a very boring film."

I stop talking about *Mr. Driver*, and study the young women to see whether my explanation of the film can interest them. I feel relaxed when I see their interest in my words.

"Thank you for your patient explanation," the young woman in the blue uniform says.

"Thank you for your patient listening," I say.

The other young woman in the grey uniform lifts her right hand and says, "I have some more questions, sir."

I repeat her words in my mind. I am too bored to answer questions. I am not sure whether I am telling the truth or not.

Sometimes I believe that I am telling the truth. Sometimes I doubt my words. Sometimes I doubt even *Mr. Driver and* Mr. Driver. I know I should not let them know this.

"OK, you can ask," I reply. "But the questions should be easy ones. If they were difficult questions, I would pretend not to hear them."

I say and they laugh. They can feel that I am kidding her.

"I learnt that you encountered some hardships in making *Mr. Driver*."

"Yes, many hardships. First, the first scriptwriter died in a car accident before finishing the script. And the second scriptwriter did not work well. We sensed that he taught us a lesson. We had no idea why. He did not finish the script. We took it back and assigned the task to another scriptwriter, who rewrote it. Finally, he finished it within six months."

"Oh, a good story of hardships," the questioner concludes.

"In truth, it is just the beginning of the story," I say. "The following parts of the story are more interesting."

"More interesting?"

I nod.

"At the very beginning, *Mr. Driver* met with several hardships. But we never thought about giving up. We did our best. The Board of Movie Censorship did not give us permission to make the movie *Mr. Driver*. The only reason was that it can be a threat to the established laws of our society and youth. And we explained the real concept of the film to the Board of Movie Censorship. Finally, the Board gave us the permission to make the movie. Indeed this is a very brief account of what we experienced. It took nearly two years to get permission."

"Is *Mr. Driver* a threat to the established laws of society as the members of the Board of Censorship thought?"

"No, not at all. It is just a challenge."

"If so, why did they ban the script of the movie? Was it according to the censorship law?"

"No, not according to censorship laws, but according to their law."

"What does *their law* mean?"

"Sorry, I don't know what it means, but I know how it works. Their own law depends on their mood. And their mood depends on what you present them."

"Oh, I see!" she exclaims suddenly, in a loud voice, and with a very surprised expression on her face.

"We all tried our best to get permission. We used various means. We used various ways. The result was that we got permission to make it into a movie."

"Do you mean that something powerful could turn the members of censorship board into a good mood?"

"Exactly, something powerful," I say. "This is not the end, you know, hardships might be the sign of *Mr. Driver*. In every step, we met with difficulties. We could all overcome every barrier. Fortunately, we could finish our task. Unfortunately, it did not meet with success. But we were all satisfied with what we had done. Time files. It happened five years ago. A five-year period is a very short period."

I stop talking. It is a very brief account of what we underwent. And I feel that what I have said about our experiences in making *Mr. Driver* can't cover our real story. I should tell her about our story in more detail than what I have explained. It is not because I can't remember those events, just because I suppose that we don't have enough time. I decide that I will tell her everything about our experiences when time and space permit us.

When all these happened to me five years ago, I was depressed, I was helpless. I felt that I was born at wrong time and in the wrong space. I lost my way. I found myself in the wilderness. I had no future. I had no hope. I ask myself whether I should tell my interviewers about these things as well.

My thoughts are interrupted by the voice of the young woman in the pink uniform.

"Can you tell me why *Mr. Driver* met with failure?" Her tone of voice and manner tell me that she has gotten the answer. The question is just to confirm her view.

"Wrong time, wrong place," I reply. I notice that my answer is too short. And I fear that she might think I get annoyed now.

I don't have any other way of saying. I say as I believe. If she is angry with me, I will apologize to her. That's all I can do. I check her expression. It is normal. I detect no sign of negative emotions, which relieves me much.

I meditate on my words. And I find that I have no reason to feel remorse for those words. I told the truth.

"I agree with you," the young woman in the pink uniform says.

I can't imagine why she says this word only after a few minutes. Was she asking herself whether she should or not?

"I am glad to know that you agree with me," I confess.

She says nothing. The other interviewers, too, say nothing. They all seem to have no more questions to ask me. When they are silent, the whole room is silent.

A camera operator walks towards the young woman in the blue uniform and shoots her while she is writing something on her laptop. I want to know what she is writing. She might be the youngest in their group. She has curly hairs, bright eyes, and an oval-shaped face. She does not speak much. She listens to what the others say and keeps on writing on her laptop. She types very fast. Amid our conversation, she can focus her mind on her business of typing. From this we can judge that she can control her mind well. She can command her mind well to concentrate on the object she wants to. I can't help but admire her power of concentration.

"Things we experience in our life test us," she says.

Her tones of voice seems like a philosopher's, I feel.

"I agree with you," I say. "And whenever I encountered such a test, I tried to encourage myself by reading fables. Fables give me strength."

"The same is true for me," the young woman in the pink uniform intervenes. "My grandpa was a good storyteller. He always told me fables. Only when I grew up, I realize that the strength in my mind and heart came from those fables."

And our conversation changes its topic. We talk about the importance of fables and parables and the intellectual challenge in our society. We talk about how we were shaped by fables told by our grandparents.

"My uncle was an avid reader. He told me many stories, tales, fables, and parables," I say. "And I had a good memory, so I remember everything he told me. I also have creative power. Even when I was about eight or nine, I was a good storyteller."

"Wow! Incredible!" they scream in unison.

"Even now I am telling you *a story*, a very good story."

They look at each other. Then they look at me. They appear to see something in me. And I appear to see something in them.

We all burst into laughter in unison. And we feel free and fresh. Our laughter fills the entire big room.

Chapter VI
With No Thought in It

Why don't I try to escape this fucking mess? This question is crawling in my mind, hissing.

I never used such a foul language. I always condemn those who use foul language. I always feel shame even to hear such a bad language. My mother shaped me to be a polite guy. She did not like using abusive or foul language. When I was a child, I used foul language. The elders taught me how to abuse. I, being a bright child, could learn easily and quickly. And they were very satisfied with my great language talent. I had a good memory, too. And so could keep every abusive word in my memory and use them any time whenever I was requested by elders. Although I could remember those bad words, I did not know what they meant. Even when I use the expression 'fuck you', I did not really know what it meant. That expression is nothing different from the words 'Dad', 'Mom' etc. So I did not feel guilty, though I used those bad words. Instead, I was even proud (even though I did not know what the word 'proud' meant, I was proud) of performing my duty. What's more I felt happy, for the elders were on my side.

In this way, I became famous for my skill in performing my great job. The news of my great fame reached my mother's ears. She, however, did not believe what she heard. So she asked me whether I really abused. With no sense of guilt, I said yes (I never lied, especially, to my mother). And she beat me with a small stick. My mother's business of beating me included questions and answers.

"Do you know why I beat you?" she asked.

I know why because she herself explained to me that I was guilty of using foul language.

"Yes, I do, Mom. It is because I used foul language."
"You confess that you are guilty, do you?"
"Yes, I do, Mom."

I gave an answer to my mother. My mother gave a beat to me. Then another question came.

"I have told you not to use foul language, haven't I?"

In fact, she failed to explain to me what foul language is and failed to give example words, expressions, and sentences of foul language.

"Yes, you have, Mom."

And I received a beating.

She asked another question.

"And you did promise that you would not, didn't you?"
"Yes, I did, Mom."
"You did not keep your promise, did you?"
"No, I did not, Mom."

Once my sentence ended, her stick fell on my hip.

She paused a few minutes. Then she asked me a question to confirm an agreement.

"Will you use such foul language later?"
"No, Mom. I will never use such foul language."

She stopped beating. I stopped abusing. I never broke my promise later.

If I really uttered the abusive word 'fucking', surely I would have broken my promise. If I still kept my promise, I would not have uttered such an abusive word. Did I break my promise? If it is certain that I did not break my promise, it would be someone else who uttered those words. Does this suggest that I am no longer I? It is impossible. I am I. I am not someone else. The evidence is that I am asking myself questions and I am criticizing myself. All these illustrate that I am I, because I have such a habit. It is, therefore, hard to say that I am someone else. If I were someone else, I would not ask questions like that, I would not analyze myself like that.

I urgently need a person who can judge the truth. He or she must be honest and righteous. He or she should not be someone who will hide something they want to. He or she should be a confidant or a confidante.

I am aware that I feel annoyed and restless. I should be calm so that I can survey the whole situation objectively. My mind must be concentrated and clear to figure out what is wrong in my mind and in what I encounter.

"Have you ever doubted your experience?"

I feel as if I have been woken up from a long sleep. I can't believe what I have heard. The question shocks me. I have never asked myself like that. Surely, I never doubted my experience. But it is just before I have heard her question. Now I begin to doubt my experience. This means that I begin to doubt my sensory perception too. OK. What is the answer to her question?

The questioner is the young woman in the blue uniform. She is waiting for my answer, not as an interviewer. She does not look like an interviewer now. When she asked the question a few seconds ago, she looked like a dishonest officer at the court. And now she looks like a dishonest judge, who is going to make a wrong decree.

What will happen to me if I answer that I never doubted my experience? What if I give the opposite answer? I am silent. I ask myself while fear overwhelms me. Though I am not brave, I am not cowardly. I never doubted my experience. That's my answer. I never doubted my experience.

"I never doubted my experience," I reply.

She looks at me and says, "You gave the same answer in an interview two or three years ago. So you still believe in your experience till now, do you?"

"My answer is yes."

She shrugs her shoulders and writes down something in her laptop. Now she looks like an interviewer.

I hear her typing.

"I had hoped you would give me a different answer," she says, in a thoughtful manner.

"Why?"

"Because you told me that sensory perceptions are not reliable. Besides, you told me that our experience can sometimes deceive us."

"Did I really tell you like that?"

"I swear, you did."

"When?"

"Last month."

If I remember correctly, I was in a village last month. I stayed there for over forty days. So it is unreasonable that I had a conversation with her last month.

"Sorry, I was in my friend's village last month."

"Maybe just before you went to the village, I suppose."

"Are you sure?"

"Yes, I am. I have a habit of writing in a diary."

"Do you mean that you wrote what we talked that day in your diary?"

"I recorded some important things."

"Can you tell me the exact date?"

"3rd July."

"Maybe I was on the way to my friend's village."

"We were having a conversation in Café Dream in the morning. So it might be in the afternoon or in the evening that you were on the way to your friend's village."

Who is the liar? She or me?

I am sure I was on the way that morning. She is sure I was with her in a café that morning. Are both of us right? On that morning, I was in the café with her, and at the same time I was on the way.

"I can't imagine who is right," I say, shaking my head desperately.

"You don't think I am telling a lie, do you?"

I shake my head. "I am just baffled," I reply. "Certainly, something is wrong."

"Okey-dokey," she says, waving her hands. "Let's go back to our topic."

I nod willingly. I also don't want to think about something unthinkable. I don't like difficult questions and mysterious subjects. I like simplicity. But sometimes the simplest thing is found to be the strangest thing.

"I have no interest in mysterious things," I say, without any particular reason. "I have no idea why."

"But you cannot shun the mysterious events in your life," she says, in a manner of knowing everything about my life.

"I know," I say. "I can't shun any event—good or bad, simple or mysterious—in my life. I can't stop it. All I can do is deal with it, no matter whether I want to or not."

"You've underwent mysterious events in your life, haven't you?"

"To be honest, I've."

"How many events?"

"I am afraid. I don't remember."

"So, many?"

"No, just a few."

"Can you tell me some?"

"Of course I can," I say. "When I was about six or seven, I was in the market with my mother, who was buying something for me. Meanwhile, my mind went back to my home. I saw my uncle at my home. And I told my mother, 'Mom, uncle is at our home.' My mother did not believe in what I told her. But when she saw my uncle having a conversation with my father, she was surprised."

"How did you see him?"

"I don't know. I just saw him."

"Did you fall asleep?"

"I was standing by my mother in the market."

"While standing by your mother, maybe you fell asleep, I think," she says, checking the expression on my face. What do you think?"

"I have no idea what it was."

"While you were standing by your mother, did your mind go back home?"

"That is what I assume. I am not sure. Sometimes, I found it hard to distinguish fact and fiction." I pause and study her. I notice that her expression changes visibly at once. I have no idea what it refers to. I, however, sense something unusual.

She seems to notice that I noticed her change of expression. She tries to hide her real feelings and emotions. She smiles at me and says, "Do you think it is mysterious that you became an actor?"

I have no answer to this question. It makes no sense, I think.

The room falls into silence again.

"To admit, I doubt the fact that I am here," I break the silence.

Heads turn to me. All cameras are focused on me.

They all focus their attention on what I am going to say. They all seem to fear that they might miss even a single word I am about to say.

"I don't believe in," I begin, "the fact that I am having this conversation with you."

I pause to think. Then I continue, "I see you. I hear you. But I can't believe. I can't believe my eyes. I can't believe my ears. I am not sure whether I really see and hear or whether I imagine that I see and hear."

"You think that your sensory perception is unreliable, don't you?"

I hesitate to say yes or no. I don't doubt my sensory perception, but my words imply that I doubt my sensory perception. I must tell her what I doubt. First, I must know what I doubt. Do I doubt my mind? Do I doubt my body? Do I doubt what I doubt?

I do not doubt my sensory perception. I doubt my presence. I doubt what I experience. I doubt my identity.

"I can't imagine how to explain," I say, frowning. "I suppose I should think hard."

The young woman in the pink uniform nods her head. "I understand you."

Why does she say so? I try to find out the answer. I fail. I don't give up. I think and think and think.

This way of thinking is mine. I am sure. I have a habit of thinking and analyzing everything in a critical way. I inherited this habit from my uncle on my mother's side, who was a good critical thinker and a good critical reader. He had to quit school in his childhood, but he read a lot. He had a passionate interest in philosophy. He influenced me so much. He encouraged me to think. He encouraged me to read. He encouraged me to live life.

One day when we were talking about literature, he said, "Thinking is an art."

At that time, I was about fifteen. I had already been a book bug. I started to enjoy reading.

"Our education does not teach us how to think and analyze. Our education only teaches us to memorize. So to speak, our education teaches us to be lazy, to be idiotic, not to be alert, not to be curious. In other words, our education kills our curiosity. That is the greatest weak point. You can't rely on our education for the art of thinking. You must rely on yourself. You yourself must develop the habit of thinking critically."

I find myself telling my interviewers about my uncle. They are all interested in what I am telling. My uncle was an ordinary man who led an ordinary life. He never told me about fame. He never told me about how Bogyoke Aung San was famous. He told me how Bogyoke Aung San struggled to gain independence for our country. He never told me how Albert Einstein was famous. He told me how Albert Einstein worked hard.

"My uncle was my teacher, my guide, my mentor. He taught me how to read. He taught me how to analyze. After I had read a book, I had to tell him about the book in brief. Then I had to give an explanation about how I see the book.

"He never told me that my view or judgment on the book was wrong. He always told me about his view on the book, saying, 'Okay, that's your view. This is mine.' I came to see later that my uncle taught me to pay respect to others' views, too."

"We may have different views on the same writing, on the same book," the young woman in the blue uniform remarks.

"Our lifestyles differ. Our social backgrounds differ. So our ways of seeing things differ," the young woman in the pink uniform explains. "When we read a piece of writing, all these things matter."

"I agree," the young woman in the grey uniform interrupts.

"So we approach it from different angles," the young woman in the pink uniform continues to explain. "So what we see differs from what others see."

"We have different styles of life, different social backgrounds," the young woman in the blue uniform says. "So it is not strange that we have different ways of seeing things."

"And in my view, we should accept the fact that we may have different ways of seeing and different ways of judging," the woman in the pink uniform says in an energetic manner.

"Your words remind me of the moral of an ancient Indian folklore *Six Blind Men and an Elephant*," says the young woman in the red uniform. "In the folklore, the wise man made the fight and argument among the six blind men end by saying: 'All of you are right.' And the question is: Who is the wise person among us. Surely we need someone who, like the wise man in the folklore, can say 'All of you are right.'" She pauses to look at the young woman in in the pink uniform, and asks: "Are you the wise person?"

The young woman in the pink uniform shakes her head immediately and screams: "No, no. I am not such a person." Then she points to the young woman in the grey uniform and says, "It might be her."

"Me?" the young woman in the grey uniform exclaims, pointing at herself with her right forefinger.

"Yes, it is you," the young woman in the pink uniform replies, with a little smile on her face.

The young women point at each other and appoint each other as the wise person. Then they stop their game of *wise person* and laugh in unison. The camera operators and others join in the laughter. So do I. I can't help laughing. I don't know why.

To laugh at their words, it is necessary to have knowledge about the *Six Blind Men and an Elephant*. In that fable, it was the wise person who could make an agreement among six blind men end. In truth, this Indian folklore has been retold in many languages and adopted in many cultures, so almost everyone who reads fables has knowledge of this folklore.

I had already read some books of fables even in my childhood. My uncle had so many books of fables, and he persuaded me to read those books.

"My uncle was good, not only to me but to the other children. It was because of his encouragement that some of us became critical readers. He always said: 'Reading is good. Reading with a critical mind is better. Reading in an abstract way is the best.' At that time, I was a boy. So his words were a mystery to me."

"You are very lucky to have such a good uncle," the young woman in the red uniform says. "I don't have such a good uncle. I envy you."

I don't know why I am telling them about my uncle. Is it because I want to boast? Or is it because I want to warn them that I know who and what I am, that I remember everything in my past, and that it is not easy to deceive me into thinking that I am someone else? Or is it just because I want them to know who my uncle was? I don't have any special purpose, do I?

I stop thinking, because I am tired of thinking. I relax myself. I am aware that it is difficult to focus my mind on something. My mind is wavering like a wayward wind. I find it hard to control my mind now. My mind is restless now. It is strange. A few minutes ago, my mind was balanced. I have no idea what turned my balanced mind into an unbalanced mind at once within a few minutes. Does this mean I don't belong to my mind? Does this mean that I am in someone else's mind?

I imagine that I should consult someone about my crisis. Someone I consult must be my confidante. I am in a dilemma over whom I should consult. I sense that everyone in this room is hiding their real identity and pretending to be someone else. All of them are disguising. I don't know who and what they really are. Therefore, it is impossible to consult one of them.

I feel as if I am lonely, helpless, powerless, and small, which beckons depression, inferiority, lack of self-confidence, and restlessness. I am in a wide room with others, at the same time I am in a narrow dark room with no one. When did this start? When will this end? This started without my knowledge. Certainly, this will end without my knowledge. What is my role in this? Is my role lost? Is even my being lost?

I must consult someone. I must confide my crisis to someone. The problem is that I sense a lack of a confidante in this room.

"I don't have an uncle," the young woman in the grey uniform says. "So I don't know what is like to have an uncle. My mother was the only child. My father only had sisters, one younger sister and three elder sisters. I have never seen my aunts. My father never told me about his sisters," our story teller pauses to study me and others. She continues, with a confident smile (maybe it is a crooked smile).

"It was from my mother that I came to learn the love story of my parents. My mother's family was poor. My dad's family was rich. So his mother forced my father not to marry my mother. My father married my mother against her will. The result was that he was not only ostracized, but disinherited by his mother as well."

It is a good story. I say in my mind. Really, it is a good story with a happy ending. Why is she telling me that story? To prevent me from thinking about the present, about the mess, about myself, about them? She fails. Her attempt to prevent me from thinking about these things fails. My mind goes on working its business. My critical thinking machine goes on running.

"One day my mother told me about my aunts, 'They are good. They love their brother so much. But they all are afraid of their mother. They don't dare do anything against their mother's will.' My mother's words left me feeling sorry for my aunts."

Her voice sinks. It is a very good action. The others stay silent, which means that they are all enchanted by her good story, by her good action. Maybe, I am the only one who is free from being enchanted by her good story, by her good action. Maybe, it is because I am the one who doubts everything, including the words, truth, reality, justice etc. Among a very few friends of mine, I am notorious for my divergent way of seeing things. I never felt sorry for this.

"My mother believes in destiny. I remember what she told me once: 'We have our own destiny. We cannot change our destiny.' I am not sure whether I believe in destiny like my mother. But I know well that some events in my life were what happened to me against my will."

She pauses.

I think. I think about the expression 'against my will.' I must confess many things happened to me against my will. That's true.

"I had a car accident," she continues her story. "My friend died on the spot in that accident. I survived. It was against my will. I did not plan to have a car accident. I did not plan to survive the accident. It is a miracle that I survived. What I want to know is: Who did it?" the young woman gives a long sigh.

I sense that she is acting. Her voice and the expression on her face are tinged with sadness. She is a good actor, which overwhelms everyone, excluding me.

After a few seconds pause, she adds, "I don't want to blame anyone or anything for such a misfortune. I inherited this attitude from my mother. She could stand fast through any hardships. She never forgot her friend, my youngest aunt. 'Your youngest aunt and I were best friends,' my mother said. 'We were the same age. We are three years younger than your dad. I always paid a visit to her home some weekends. And your dad and I became familiar. Your dad never had interest in a love affair. I was beautiful, but it could not attract him at all. He was handsome, but it could not attract me at all. He was a quiet man. He loves reading more than girls and anything else. He did not show any sign of interest towards me. It was impossible for us to be lovers without his youngest sister's attempts. She loved me so much. So she wanted me to be her sister-in-law. I never imagined that your dad would be my husband. Destiny is very mysterious. He fell in love with me. But I did not know what love was. I thought that I did not love him. As I have said, your aunt and I were best friends. I did not want to neglect her wish. And I said yes. It was only after some years later, after our marriage that I fell in love with your dad. And I thanked to your aunt for her attempts. None of us—your dad, your aunts, and I—knew what would happen to us after our marriage. None of us foresaw that your dad would be ostracized and disinherited: none of us foresaw the detriment to our marriage.' When I heard this, I felt something mysterious. I do not see my grandmother as a villain. So, who is the villain? One of my aunts? My dad? My mom? No one is the villain, I think. Who or what is responsible for this?"

I don't like her story. I don't think her story is true. But I feel something true in the story. To be honest, I don't believe in destiny. Sometimes I see that destiny is something on which we blame our failure. In other words, destiny is something very helpful for our escape from our responsibility.

"My mother was a thinker, too. Of their marriage, she says, 'Our marriage was a detriment to your grandparents' family. Due to our marriage, their happy family broke. But our marriage might be a bonus to our family. Now, we have a happy family with three good, dutiful daughters.' My mother is right. Our family leads a happy life. I am not sure whether it is a bonus just like my mother commented."

She stops telling her story.

No one asks her about her aunts and about her grandparents and about her sisters. From what she told, we know that her paternal grandmother did not want her son to marry a poor girl. We do not know about her maternal grandparents and her paternal grandfather. She did not tell us about them. Why not?

As I have admitted, I have no interest in her story. She told the story only in order to divert attention from the mess. She excels at diverting attention. Her weak point is that she underestimates me. She does not know that I know what she is doing.

"Wow!" I exclaim. That's all I say. I really want to say is: "You should write stories. I dare to bet that you will be a good writer." I try to suppress my desire. I fear that she will get an inkling that I distrust her. I can act well. She does not suspect me of acting.

"I know well that you are a good actor," she says, with a mysterious smile on her face.

I can't guess the meaning of her words and of her smile. Does it mean that she knows I am pretending or that she knows I have excellent skills by acting in films? Both her words and smile carry a sense of ambiguity.

I try to cut off the thought process. I don't fail this time.

A strange thought occurs. It is about my mind and my body. As the very first time (maybe it is the second time or the third time), I doubt my body. I am warned that this is not my body, and that my mind accesses someone else's body.

This thought drags me somewhere far in the past.

It was summer holidays. I was about twelve or thirteen. I paid a visit to my father's village with my mother. We stayed there for four weeks, spending time with my cousins. The two or three days before we left the village, I witnessed a miracle there, in my father's native village. Though it was a miracle to me, to my relatives and other villagers, it was not a miracle. It was something normal they always saw and heard. I never believed that it was real. Now my view changes: I think it might be real. My poor knowledge, my poor education could not follow it. That's why I drew an easy conclusion that it was not real.

What I saw and heard was this.

A young beautiful girl of about fifteen (later I came to know that she was my second cousin who was two years older than me) was amid the crowd, a man of sixty was uttering some words so quietly that I could not hear him utter. I, however, heard the girl's voice. Sometimes she abused, sometimes she made strange voices, sometimes she wept. She was a very polite girl. She was a very modest girl. She was a very quiet girl. She was a beautiful girl. Her original state of mind disappeared. Her original behavior disappeared. Her original features disappeared. What we saw was not her face. It was an ugly, distorted face. Her beautiful eyes were no more beautiful. They were red with anger, with aggression, and with barbarity.

"She is bewitched," a woman explained. "The spirit of a witch accessed her mind."

I could not follow what she said.

She was convinced that I was not convinced. So she tried to explain in other way: "Now her mind is no more hers. It is accessed by an evil spirit of a witch."

Her explanation was still a mystery to me.

She pointed to the man uttering something we could not hear, and said, "Now that man is driving the witch's spirit out of her mind."

"What is he?"

"He is a man who has psychic power. He can expel evil spirits."

"What is 'psychic power'?" I asked.

"It is something special. Ordinary people have no such powers."

More complicated. "And what's 'evil spirit'?"

"It is something bad. It can control our minds. Once your mind is controlled with its power, your mind is no longer your mind. You will do bad things which you have never done before. You are no longer you."

Her painstaking explanation did not help. I was still perplexed.

Psychic powers, evil spirits: all were beyond my knowledge. I had never heard those things before. So I did not know what they meant. Who knows what is beyond his knowledge? I did not learn those things in school. I did not learn those things from the elders. So I had no knowledge about them. So I did not understand what the woman explained to me.

"Do you think he will save the girl?" I asked.

"Of course, he can," the woman guaranteed. "His psychic power is very amazing. He can control the witches well. Wait and see. The witch will plead him."

A few minutes later, the girl stopped abusing. She was exhausted.

The man asked, "Why do you bewitch the girl?"

The girl answered something. I did not hear well. But I noticed well that that was not the girl's voice. It was the voice of an old woman.

"The girl is speaking like an old woman," I said.

"It is not the girl who is speaking," the woman explained. "It is the old woman, the old witch."

The man threw some drops of water onto the girl body. The girl cried and pleaded to stop throwing drops of water at her.

"Why is she crying and pleading," I asked the woman.

"She feels hot."

"She feels hot. Why?"

"Drops of water are hitting her."

"Is it boiling water?"

"No, not boiling water."

"I can't imagine why water makes her feel hot."

"Even drops of water are fire to her."

"Why are the drops of water fire to her?"

"Because of the man's psychic power."

I asked. The woman answered. But I was still bewildered. The language was strange. The subject was unfamiliar.

The man stopped throwing water. The girl stopped yelling.

The man put a bowl of water in front of the girl.

"Look into the water," he told the girl.

The girl did as ordered. She was shocked.

"What do you see?" the man asked.

"I see... I see..." The girl could not finish her sentence.

"You see what?"

"A face," the girl answered fearfully. "A very grotesque face." The girl's voice was shaking.

"Have you ever seen this face?"

"Yes, sir. I've."

"So you know whose face it is, don't you?"

"Yes, I do."

"Keep it a secret. Don't tell anyone what you see now. Promise?"

"Yes, I promise."

Dialogue between the man and the girl ended. This meant that the man had driven out the evil spirit of the witch successfully.

"You are right. The man has saved the girl," I said.

"This is not the first time I witness that he can cure such patients."

I changed the topic.

"Whose face does she see in the water bowl?" I asked the woman.

The woman shook her head. "I don't know."

"And do the others by her also see it?"
"No one but she can see."
"Why?"
"I don't know."
"You always say, 'I don't know'."
"There are many things I don't know."
"The girl will keep it a secret all the time."
"Certainly, she will."
"And you don't know why she will, do you?"
The woman smiles at me. "You are right."
"Can the girl remember what she did while she was being bewitched?" I asked the woman.
"No, she can't."
"Why not?"
"It was not she who did those things. She was being witched."
"Is there a way for her to remember those things?"
The woman shook her head. "I don't know."

It was the first and the last time I had ever seen such a miracle that one's mind can access the other's body and mind. What I experience now differs from what my second cousin experienced. She was bewitched. Her mind was accessed by someone. Now I am not bewitched. I am bewitching someone. My mind is not accessed by someone. I have accessed someone's mind and body. But it is hard to say I have bewitched someone, because I don't try to control someone with magic or psychic power. To be more exact, I don't try to access someone's mind. My mind is in someone's body, without my knowledge. That's all I can explain. I have no idea how to explain more clearly.

If I told someone about this feeling of mine, I surely would be regarded to be mentally ill. And I would be sent to the mental hospital to cure my mental illness. I am sure I am not mad. I am just thinking that my mind is in someone's body and mind. My mind did not intrude into someone's body and mind. My mind was put into someone's body and mind without my knowledge, without my consent. This might be a well-planned plot. I don't know who did this. I, however, can swear that I am not a catalyst for this. I am just a prey. I have been framed.

What a ridiculous thing!

"Can we restart our conversation?" the young woman in the grey uniform asks after a brief silence, a brief silence for thoughts.

I don't remember where our conversation ended. Forgetting or remembering does not matter now. What matters now is what it signifies: my memory starts to break down. That's too bad. I depend on my memory to check everything I witness. How can I rely on the broken-down memory?

We are having a conversation at random. So the subjects are changing all the time. The result is that we don't remember what the original subject of our conversation is. Even this might be a part of the plan. That's what I guess. Who can confirm that it is not a well-planned conversation? Who knows its programmer?

"Nothing happens without a plan," the young woman in the pink uniform says.

"Majority happens according to a plan," I correct her. "We have to act as planned. We have no right to change any part of the plan."

"Nothing happens without a plan," she says the same words, with stern expression on her face. It is certain she feels indignant.

She takes a piece of paper and a ballpoint pen. Then she writes SIGHT on it. And then she shows all of us and says: "We can see these words."

I know what she will do next.

She beckons a boy and hands him the sheet.

The boy is about seventeen. He is a student of a private film school. He is very obedient and hard-working.

"Can you stick this paper on that wall?" she says, pointing to the wall, which is fifteen feet distant.

"Yes, madam," the boy replies. He is standing straight, with his hands at his both sides. His manner is like a well-trained, obedient soldier, who is ready to obey the order of his officer.

"After you've stuck it onto the wall, raise your right hand, please." She raises her right hand.

The boy nods and walks to the wall, with the sheet of paper in his right hand. He takes graceful paces towards the wall. It is as though he is carrying a national flag at the opening ceremony of independent day.

A few seconds later, we see the boy raise his right hand gracefully.

We see a faint shape of the sheet of paper on the wall, but we can't see the word SIGHT on it. What we see blurs.

I know well beforehand what and how she will explain to us.

She looks at everyone and asks: "Now can you see the word SIGHT on the sheet?"

We all shake our heads in unison, like primary school students do when they don't know the answer of their respected female teacher's question. We don't see the word. The paper blurs.

She continues, "Surely, the paper is there on the wall. The word SIGHT is there on the paper. We, however, can't see it. Why? It is simple. Our sight has its limitation. We can see things near. But we can't see things far." She pauses.

She pauses to study her audience. She sees her audience's deep interest, and she feels satisfied.

"Our eyes can see things within our sight," she adds. "We can't see things beyond our sight. Eyesight may differ from each other. So the thing within your eyesight might be the thing beyond the other's eyesight."

We are being enchanted by her lecture. The room is silent. We are listening carefully as though we fear that we would miss even a word from her lecture. All of us, not excluding me, focus on her.

"Here is the same. Our intellectual sight has its limitation. How and what we see thorough our intellectual eyes is within limit. Some events appear to happen without any plan. We think so, because our intellectual sight can't follow it or it is beyond our intellectual sight. The plan we see is the word SIGHT on the paper in front of us. The plan we don't see is the word SIGHT on the paper on the wall which is about fifteen feet distant."

Her theory is reasonable.

"We can classify distance into two: physical distance and intellectual distance. Distance between the place where we are sitting and the wall on which the sheet of paper is stuck is physical distance. But distance between our intellect and the plan is intellectual distance. Physical distance is visible. But intellectual distance is invisible. Such distance depends on the degree of eyesight. Physical distance relies on physical eyesight. Intellectual distance relies on intellectual eyesight.

"We conclude that some events happen without any plan. This conclusion relies on our intellectual distance. If the intellectual distance is narrow enough to see the plan, we will not draw such a conclusion."

No one comments. Her lecture leaves everyone meditative.

The topic of our recent conversation comes back to me. It is about destiny.

"We have talked about destiny," the young woman in the red uniform reminds us. "It is a very interesting subject."

"Don't forget to put the adjective 'controversial' before it," the young woman in the blue uniform warns.

"Thank you for your warning," the young woman in the red uniforms says. She really thanks the young woman in the blue uniform. Destiny is a very controversial subject, too.

I don't want to accept the theory that once I was born, I had been shaped to be a certain type of man. Even before I learn about art, was it certain that I would be an artist? Is my choice of subject related to my destiny? Would everything push me to be an actor if I was destined to be an actor? Would everything drive me to be a writer if I was destined to be a writer? Is it because of my destiny that I made great efforts? Is it because of my destiny that I never gave up my decision? Is my destiny related to anything I do? Is even the business of breathing in and breathing out related to my destiny? Is even my interest in something related to my destiny?

Sometimes something bad happened to me against my will. And I could not help asking myself: Is it a mysterious power which made it? I don't want to believe in such a mysterious power which can govern one's life and events. But I can't neglect the fact there are events—good or bad—which happened without our involvement. Those were the decisive events for our lives, but we did not know beforehand that they would happen to us. Were those events connected to mysterious powers or destiny? Or were those events connected to something else? Now I am in this room without my involvement. I did not enter this room. I had no appointment to meet someone in this room. I had no plan to have a conversation in this room. Anyway, I find myself in this room with others. Why? Is this a part of my destiny? Is this what created by destiny?

Is destiny a closed book with invisible pages? Though I asked questions, I never got any answer. Strangely, I never gave up questioning. I still believe that there is a right answer for all questions. The problem is that we lack knowledge, intellect, and effort which are perfect enough to find out right answers. And the easiest way is to say, like a lazy person: 'there is no answer.'

My mind goes back to the subject of destiny. Everything is a mystery before we can find out the secret about it. Similarly, destiny will remain a mystery as long as we can't uncover its secret. Even the speed of light was a mystery because scientists could not discover its secret. I suppose that one day the secret of destiny will surely be uncovered. Then destiny will no longer be a mystery.

I change my position. I sit upright. I try to drive out drowsiness. Probably I will fall asleep within a few minutes. I must be alert so that I can plan to go out of this mess.

"We all thank you," the young woman in the blue uniform says.

I hoped that she or the other young woman will restart the conversation with the subject of destiny.

"For what?" I ask.

"For your arrangement with us to have a conversation."

"Pardon me," I say.

"Two days ago we talked about this conversation on the phone."

My memory keeps no information about this telephone conversation with her. Probably, she is telling me a lie. Probably, she is making me a fool. She should realize that I am not the type of person who can be fooled easily.

It becomes more complicated. Her explanation leaves me muddled. The more I think, the more I feel bewildered. Did I really talk about this with her on phone two days ago? If I really had a talk with her on phone, then the call would be logged in my phone.

I try to go back to the two-day past. I don't see many events. I see myself having a conversation with someone on phone. I can't imagine what I was talking. I can't imagine with whom I was talking. I notice that the expression on my face was serious. From this I can say that we were talking about something serious.

Okay, what is something serious? Was it about this conversation?

I feel that I should take a walk in the room to refresh my memory. My memory is crammed with trivial things. I must delete some of them. While taking a walk, I can find out a way out, I suppose.

"I think I should take a walk in this room," I say.

The young woman in the red uniform smiles at me, saying, "Of course, you should. But we should not stop talking midway through our conversation."

I am not sure whether her word is an advice or a warning, an order or a threat. From the expression on her face, it can be judged that she is giving an advice. But from her tone of voice, it can be judged that she is giving a command.

"We have talked for hours," I reason. "So we should take rest for a moment."

She shrugs her shoulders, and replies, "Yes, we should. But we shouldn't."

I say nothing. Nothing I have to say.

"This conversation is very important for you," she explains in low tone, pretending to be patient. "You should focus your mind on the conversation only."

Does this suggest that she knows I did not focus my mind fully on the conversation? I must admit that sometimes my mind wandered. But why is this conversation important to me? By important, what does she mean? Serious? Decisive?

"I admit that sometimes I failed to focus my mind on the conversation," I confess.

She glances around the room and says, lowering her voice, as if she might be overheard: "We should be aware of."

Aware of what? I ask myself. No answer. Does she warn me indirectly that we are being watched or our conversation is being watched? Watched by whom? Watched by what?

I feel slightly restless. So I try to calm myself down. It is hard. I fail.

"Okey-dokey, can you tell me how did you overcome hardships?"

"Many hardships in my life," I start my story. "It is not unusual to overcome hardships, I suppose.

"The first hardship in my life started as a fight against the orders of my family. My parents and my siblings wanted me to be an educated person—an engineer, an architect, a medical doctor etc. So they tried to mold me as they liked. My parents were famous physicians. My elder brothers and sisters are physicians and architects. So it is not strange that they wanted me to be a physician or an architect etc. And it is not strange that I did not want to be a physician or an architect. In this way a small revolution started.

"I announced that I would do as I wanted, not as they wanted. They did not want me to be an actor. I wanted to be an actor. They believed that what they did was right. I believed that what I did was right. They did not give up. I did not surrender. The result was that I was disinherited."

I pause and study them. They show no sign of interest.

This is not the true story of mine stored in my memory, or the story of anyone, but the imaginary story in my mind. I have no idea how this story occurred to me. I invented this story to madden them.

"We all know this story," the young woman says.

What does she mean? She means that it is true story of my life, or that I have ever told this story of mine several times, doesn't she? Or they pretend not to know that this is not a true story of mine. What is certain is that unfortunately my grand plan to infuriate them fails. If my plan succeeded, they would be angry with me and tell me the true story of mine—who and what I am etc. And...

My thought process is interrupted.

"We'd like to know the other hardships in your life," she says, in patient tone, in a patient manner. But both carry the sense of strict order. "Especially we'd like to know the barriers you encountered when you started out on a career as an actor."

A very good story of an actor appears in my mind. I am not sure whether it is true or fictional. I have no option but to retell some barriers in the story.

"There are many hardships," I start. But I have no idea how to continue. The first thing I remember is this: "At that time, I was about twenty or so. My experience during the first shooting was my depression. I thought that I had no talent in acting. I felt that everyone mocked at me in the shooting. I tried to do as taught by the director, but I failed and failed. I lost self-confidence. I decided to give up my dream to be an actor."

"Can you tell me about your experience during the first shooting in detail?"

"In truth, it is something I want to drive out of my memory. Whenever I think about it, I feel ashamed."

"Don't you think that it is a driving force?"

"A driving force?"

"Yes, a driving force for you to go on trying."

"Maybe. But at that time, my only idea was to stay away from anyone, to keep myself alone in my own world, in my own den."

"Did you try to commit suicide?"

"No, I didn't. Even the thought of committing suicide did not occur to me. I just wanted to be alone."

"Why?"

"I don't know why. Maybe it is because of my destiny, I think."

"Because of destiny!" she exclaims. "Do you mean that you are destined to be an actor, so you did not try to commit suicide?"

"No, no, no," I shake my hands. "I mean that my destiny does not include committing suicide."

"I think I understand what you mean," she says, laughing lightly.

"I beg your pardon, it is my fault," I apologize. "I lack good skills in speaking clearly. Perhaps it is because I don't think clearly."

"You use the word 'destiny'. Do you believe in *destiny*?"

"By *destiny* I mean 'the forces of the deed which I performed in my previous life. This is based on the theory of kammic law and on the theory of the cycle of death and rebirth. And so it might be far-fetched. This type of destiny plays an important role in present life."

"It is mysterious," she comments.

"Yes, it is."

"Even this conversation might be a part of your destiny."

"It is hard to say absolutely no. This is the subject beyond the horizon of our knowledge and intellect. It is more mysterious than we can imagine."

"Do you want to say that we must be prophets to discuss such a mysterious subject?" the young woman in the red uniform asks, with an amusing expression on her face.

"I did not say that. You said it," I say. She laughs.

Without any reason, we all laugh in unison.

A few minutes later, the young woman in the blue uniform questions, "Now are you ready to tell us about the other difficulties in your career?"

"This subject is very boring."

"But it can give good lessons to others."

"What if the stories of hardships I am telling you are not true?"

"I don't think you will tell such things."

"But I am thinking about telling such things."

Her eyes widen as though she feels extremely astonished.

"Oh, you are planning to make fictional stories of hardships," she says amusingly.

"Exactly," I reply.

I fail to be aware of the present moment, of the present crisis, of the present mess. I am free. I am alone. I am not in the room. I am somewhere. I want this moment last longer. But I know well that this also will pass when it is time to pass, according to the theory of change: *Everything changes according to the nature of changing.*

"For everything there is a season," I say. "A time to arise and a time to pass."

In fact, I don't mean to speak these words. I just mean to whisper them inside my head.

"This reminds me of Solomon's words in Ecclesiastes," she says.

From what she says, I judge that she also reads Bible. But these words—A time to arise and a time to pass—are not from Ecclesiastes.

"Some scholars thought that Ecclesiastes was not written by King Solomon," I explain.

"However, some scholars believed that it was written by King Solomon."

"The scholars have contradictory beliefs on the authorship of Ecclesiastes," I say. "They have their own reasons: reasons for Solomon authorship and reasons for non-Solomon authorship.

The text has contradictions. The authorship of the text has contradictions. It is hard to say whose views are right and whose views are wrong."

She laughs lightly. "That is very interesting."

"What is interesting?"

"Contradiction," she replies. "I have passionate interest in contradictions."

"Why?"

"You believe that everything has an exact answer, don't you?"

"Sorry, I should not have asked that question," I apologize immediately. "Like you, I am interested in contradictions, but I don't know why."

"That is it," she exclaims, snapping her finger.

I am surprised. Young women hardly behave like this.

The other young women, too, are astonished at her behavior. It seems that this behavior is strange to them, too.

I see no sign of embarrassment on her face. Is it because she is not aware of her strange behavior? Or is it because she does not feel that it is not a strange behavior? To be honest, I never saw a girl or a young woman snap her fingers. I admit that I like this behavior of hers. I sense freedom in her behavior.

"For everything there is a season," she goes back to our recent subject suddenly. "This is true, no matter who wrote it. Maybe it was Solomon or skeptic or someone who was the wisest in the world or the other who wrote it."

"Right," I agree. "Truth is truth."

"According to this theory," she concludes, "there is a time to begin and a time to end."

There is a time to begin and a time to end. I repeat these words in my mind. Why does she speak these words? Does she say these words intentionally or unintentionally? What's her intention? *A time to end.* What does it mean?

Does it suggest that to this conversation will come to an end? Does it suggest that this mess will come to an end? I ever heard the expression 'happy ending'. Will *happy ending* come soon?

Her words leave me thoughtful.

What should I do now? Should I attack them and try to escape? Or should I wait till everything comes to an end? I have no desire to attack anyone. And no one shows any sign of hostility or aggression. Instead I see signs of friendliness, honesty, righteousness etc. on their faces. If all these signs were false, they might be imposters or frauds or double-dealers who have special skills in pretending.

"We talked about destiny," the young woman in the pink uniform says. Now she looks like a philosopher. "We talked that for everything there is a time. Do you think that these two have relationship?"

I shrug my shoulders. "Pardon me please, the question baffles me."

She remains silent for a few minutes. She is thinking hard. Perhaps, she is searching for the best example. "In 1945, the Second World War ended."

"In 1945, the Second World War ended," I echo.

"Can we say that the Second World War ended, because it was time to end?"

I have no idea what to say. There were several reasons and theories on the end of the Second World War. However, generally speaking, we can say that the Second World War ended, because it was time to end.

"To speak generally," I begin, "the Second World War ended, because it was time to end."

"Okay, is it related to destiny?"

I laugh heartily. "You chose wrong person," I say.

"No, I chose right person," she replies.

"You should ask such questions from a philosopher," I say.

She remains silent, waiting for something I will say next.

"I am not a philosopher," I explain.

She shrugs her shoulders. "Yes, I know."

"I am an actor."

Now I come to notice that I have slipped something I don't want to tell. It is too late to correct what I have said. It is impossible to take the spoken word back. I am a fool.

"Oh, I know what you are," she says.

I see a mysterious smile on her face. I know well what that it means. It has relationship with my word.

Certainly, she will not give up her idea. She may have reasons to ask me such questions. The problem is that I don't know the reasons. In other words, I have no idea why she is determined to ask me such a question.

"In 1939, the Second World War began, and in 1945, it ended. So it is certain that a war has a beginning and an ending. Are these two—the beginning and the ending—related to destiny?"

I shake my head. "Terribly sorry, I have no answer."

"No, you have an answer," she says. "You are afraid to answer."

"No, I have nothing to be afraid of." I notice that my voice is slightly louder.

"If not, you will answer."

She does not give up asking. "We are not scholars, we are not great historians. And now we are not surveying or researching," she explains patiently. "I ask you as a friend. I just want to know how you think. Don't think seriously like a scholar or a historian does, think like an actor."

She does advise.

I do think.

I ever heard someone say: *There is always a way.* This word meant nothing to me before. Now this very word means everything to me. It might be a light of hope. Into my mind I insert the thought that there is a way for me.

I am not the type of person who relinquishes easily. My bitter experiences have shaped me into a strong-minded person.

Now it is time for me to meditate on what is happening to me. Recently I doubted my mind. And now I should reflect on my doubt. No doubt that I have a habit of reflecting, pondering, contemplating on things. This habit is not the inheritance from my parents or from my grandparents. I wonder from whom I inherited this habit. Perhaps I inherited this habit from my great grandparents or from my forebears. Or I inherited this habit from no one. Maybe, this is my inborn habit. Maybe, this came from reading, education.

I am thinking. I am meditating. Thinking or meditating is the business of mind. Now I am performing businesses of mind. Therefore, it is very obvious whose mind is this. The one who is performing the business of thinking and meditating is I, so this mind is mine. No doubt. But body is someone else's. Why? I feel that I am not familiar with this body. My body is cool. This body is warm. My body is slim. This body is stout. My body has dark skinned. This body has fair skinned. On the right forearm of this body, there is a small mark of circle. On the same spot of my body, there is a huge mark circle. The same mark on the same spot, but different sizes. The mark on my body is inborn. The mark on this body is artificial.

From what I see now, to judge exactly whose mind is this is impossible. While pondering, I am aware that I feel impatient. I want to yell out loudly. I want to use foul language: shit, fuck, mother fucker, son of bitch etc. I never use foul language. I want to hurt someone. This is not the sign of my mind. This is the sign of cruel mind. My mind is mild. This type of mind is not mine. My mind is polite. My mind is patient. My mind is very kind. This mind is rude. This mind is sensitive. This mind is aggressive. I find myself meditating on all these things. This is the sign of my mind. The habit and practice of meditating on things is the habit and practice of my mind.

This is my mind. At the same time this is someone else's mind, too. This mind has two different sets: mine and someone else's. It seems that this mind belongs to two beings: to me and to someone. One mind belongs to two beings. What an incredible thing!

And body?

If so, the body can be mine. Perhaps, I mistake my body for someone else's body. Perhaps I mistake my mine for someone else's mind. Or the body also belongs to two beings: to me and to someone.

The harder I think, the further I am from the solution.

I am a car of which engine and body have different brands. No, this is the wrong metaphor. I must stop thinking for a long time.

I study my interviewers. They are busy. They have no time to ask me questions at present, I think.

I am wrong. The young woman in the red uniform says, "I forgot to say that I like your *Beyond Circle*, in which you starred as a happy philosopher."

I try to think back. In my mind, some moving pictures appear. I am not sure whether they are real or false. What I see is an interview. Someone was asking me questions and I was answering. I can't imagine where we were.

"Did you think that *Beyond Circle* would meet with success like this?"

"I am afraid. You know, it is hard to tell. I did my best. That's all."

"And now it meets with unexpected success."

"Yes, it does."

"May I know your opinion on this unexpected success?"

"To be honest, I am happy. This is a test."

These words enter my mind. My memory is not good enough to remember exact sentences with exact order of words. This might be a trap. Or this might be an illusion.

"I watched *Beyond Circle*, and liked it, though it is boring," the young woman in the red uniform says. "At that time, I was a final year university student of Burmese literature. One or two months later after I had watched the film, I came across your interview in a film magazine. I still remember the words you said, 'In fact, this is a test.' It were the words you said at the end of the interview that I liked the most."

I have nothing to say. My head is filled with the echo of THIS IS A TEST THIS IS A TEST THIS IS A TEST THIS IS A TEST THIS IS A TEST THIS IS A TEST THIS IS A TEST THIS IS A TEST THIS IS A TEST THIS IS A TEST THIS IS A TEST THIS IS A TEST THIS IS A TEST THIS IS A TEST THIS IS A TEST THIS IS A TEST THIS IS A TEST. THIS IS A TEST THIS IS A TEST THIS IS A TEST THIS IS A TEST THIS IS A TEST THIS IS A TEST. THIS IS A TEST THIS IS A TEST THIS IS A TEST THIS IS A TEST THIS IS A TEST.

Is this also a test?

The young woman in the pink uniform stops writing. Her prose is good. The first sentence on her essay on my new film can attract the reader well, I believe. Since she was a middle school girl, she proved that she has language talent and prose talent. Her first teacher of prose was a Burmese essayist. She always won first prize in essay writing in every grade. When she was at the university, she stopped taking part in the essay competition. But she never stopped writing essays. I am her essay-reader. She has not published her book of essays. Nearly thirty essays of her have already appeared in various literary magazines.

"You should publish a book of essays," I advise her.

She looks at me, with puzzled expression on her face.

"Why should I publish essay book?"

"Your essays are good."

She widens her eyes. "You mistake me for someone else. I never wrote an essay. Writing is the job I hate most."

It makes no sense that I mistake her for someone else. She herself told me about it. She has amnesia, I think. If not, she pretends to be an amnesiac. She must a reason or some reasons for this. It is not my business to try to find out the reasons why she pretends. Certainly, I can say that she is not good at pretending. She can't make me believe.

She is silent. It is certain that she has many things to say and ask. She wants to continue this conversation and I want to end this conversation. She is finding out how to restart this conversation, and I am finding out how to end up this conversation.

Now I want to look up at the sky. What time is it now? Is it morning? Is it noon? Is it afternoon? Is it evening? Is it night? Is it sunny? Is it cloudy? Is it raining? I know nothing outside. The things outside are the things from another world. The air outside is the air from another world. I don't know how many years I have breathed in the very fresh air. Now the air I breathe in here in this room is not the fresh air. It is mixed with the nice smell of air freshener. And I come to realize the value of the very fresh air, I long for the fresh air. I don't want to imagine that I will never breathe in the fresh air again. I think of the political prisoners who died in the narrow room, longing for the fresh air, which hurts me so much.

I am not sure how these walls painted light red are thick. However, I am sure that these walls are thick enough to prevent us from hearing outside things.

I hear nothing from the outside. I have no idea where I was before I am here in this room. The guy who took me into this room must know where I was then. I should find out first the guy who took me into this room. What if I entered this room with a will?

I have studied the room many times. It has no window, no door. It must have doors. The doors might be hidden with the help of high technology. I see no trace of door on the wall. If there is no door, it is impossible for us to enter this room, it is impossible for us to have conversation like this. There must be a door through which we entered. I have no memory of how I entered. In reality, I am not sure even whether I entered the room with a will or I was forced to enter the room. My word is unreasonable. In truth, what is happening to me is unreasonable, too.

Let me see something reasonable.

The room is air conditioned, and its ceiling is decorated with many light bulbs. At each point where four six-foot square sheets meet, a light bulb is installed. So the whole room is bright with light, and it is hard to distinguish whether it is day or night in the room.

I don't like the thick walls painted light red. I don't like the artificial light. I don't like air conditioning. I don't like nice smell of air freshener. I want to see natural light. I want to see natural surroundings. I want to breathe in the fresh air. I want to see people come and go. I want to hear people speaking. I want to hear people quarreling. This room is a false world, a world of pretention. I want to go out of this room as quickly as possible. The quicker, the better.

I look around the room. Everyone is busy or is pretending to be busy. Everyone appears lifeless. I notice that everyone puts Bluetooth in their right ear. The expression on everyone's face shows that they wait for the order and do as commanded via Bluetooth. Everyone is a robot, I sense.

And now I am bored by studying all of them. I am tired of looking around the room. I am fatigued by checking everything which appeared in my mind. It is time to rest.

I relax.

I breathe in and breathe out steadily. I don't make any effort to breathe in. I don't make any effort to breathe out. Time flies. Some minutes have passed. It helps. I feel better. What is the next step? Should I keep breathing in and breathing out steadily for hours?

Gradually, I become calm and restful. I start to doubt where I am. The thought that I am here in this room might be false. It might be the thing in my imagination. I create it in my imagination. Everything I experience might be something in my imagination. Things in imagination are hard to distinguish from things in the real world. This room, this conversation, everyone, everything might be a thing in my imagination. I create everything, everyone in my imagination. To get out of my imagination is to get out of this mess, to get out of this room. The crisis is that I have no idea how to get out of my imagination.

The young woman in the red uniform looks at me.

I see a mysterious smile on her face. What I see is false. The young woman is the image in my imagination. She is not real. She is a phantom.

"No one can fool me any longer," I say.

She frowns, and asks: "What are you talking about?"

I laugh. "No one can fool me any longer."

She shakes her head. She sighs. "No one fools you."

"Even now you are fooling me."

"I am fooling you. How?"

"You are not real. But you are pretending to be real."

"Something wrong, I think."

"Do you mean that I am abnormal?"

"No, I didn't use the word 'abnormal'."

"You didn't use the word, yet you said *something wrong*, didn't you."

"Oh, I see. I did."

"It has the same meaning."

The dialogue between two of us pauses.

I try to see whether this dialogue is real or false, is fact or fiction, whether I am in my imagination or I am in a real environment. I smell something nice. Damn it. It might be because my olfactory organs do not work properly. Or it might be because I am fooled by my sensory perception.

Now another question arises. Is my sensory perception reliable?

I give a long, heavy sigh.

"How can I help you?"

The young woman in the pink uniform asks.

I shake my head.

"No, thank you."

That is a lie. I need help. I need help to end this fucking mess. I need help to get out of this fucking mess. Now I have a second thought about what I did say and what I failed to say. It is time for me to make a decision. It is time to make choice.

I hear footstep from behind me. The sounds of footsteps stop. I turn back. I can't believe what I see. I am afraid that it might be an imagination. I fear to blink. When I blink, everything will change immediately from reality to imagination. I fear that such bad thing will happen.

My lover. Yes, it is my lover. I see her approaching me. She shows no sign of surprise. I try to figure out how and why she is here. Was she invited? Was she forced? I see no expression of fear on her face. So I conclude that she comes here in her will, and I feel relaxed.

I did not hope she will come. She has no courage to do something like this. Now I see her as a brave young woman. I wonder what changed her personality. It does not matter how she has changed into a brave young woman. What matters is how she will help me.

I stand up and to hold her in my arms. She steps back suddenly, with astonished expression on her face.

I am astonished to see the expression of unfriendliness on her face.

The young woman in the blue uniform introduces me with my lover.

I shrug my shoulders. "I know. She is my lover."

I notice a surprised expression on her face. I sense that she is pretending.

I can't help but laugh.

"Tell them something," I look at my lover and say. "Tell them that we are lovers."

Now I see the shock on her face.

"Oh, no, no. I am not your lover."

"You are really Miss Moon, aren't you?"

She nods.

"Yes, I am Miss Moon," she replies in complete sentence.

"Do you like mystery novels?"

"Of course, I do."

"That is it," I exclaim happily. "My lover Miss Moon likes mystery novels."

She sighs. "I am Miss Moon. I like mystery novels," she explains. "But I am not your lover. I am your designer."

I don't doubt what I sense, yet I doubt what I encounter. But my instinct convinces me that she is telling lie. I sense that she is my lover. However, on her face, I see no signs of intimacy between us. Does even my lover betray me? Does even my lover pretend to not to be my lover? She can hide real feelings and emotions. I want to ask her the reason why she feigns indifference. When she says something, she does not look at me. She, rubbing her hands, gazes somewhere, instead. This is the habit of my lover. My lover, whenever she tells me a lie, gazes somewhere, rubbing her hands.

"Why are you here?" I ask, but I know that she will tell me something untrue.

"This is a part of our plan," she says. "I am at the appointed place, at the appointed time as you told me yesterday."

In fact, I told her on phone that we would meet in the City Park today. However now she tells me something I did not really told her.

Do I forget that I told her to come here? Do I mistake her for my lover?

She says that this is a part of our plan. What is OUR PLAN?

Everyone is silent.

"Sorry, I don't mean to disturb your conversation," The young woman who calls herself Miss Moon apologizes. "Please go on."

Everyone and everything resumes.

The young women exchange looks.

"Okey-dokey," the young woman in the grey uniform announces, "let us restart our conversation." Then she gestures all, including me.

And the conversation resumes.

The End